Creeping with the Enemy

A LANGDON PREP NOVEL

KIMBERLY REID

Dafina KTeen Books
KENSINGTON PUBLISHING CORP.
http://www.kensingtonbooks.com

DAFINA KTEEN BOOKS are published by

Kensington Publishing Corp.
119 West 40th Street
New York, NY 10018

All Kensington titles, imprints and distributed lines are available at special quantity discounts for bulk purchases for sales promotion, premiums, fund-raising, educational or institutional use.

Special book excerpts or customized printings can also be created to fit specific needs. For details, write or phone the office of the Kensington Special Sales Manager. Attn.: Special Sales Department. Kensington Publishing Corp., 119 West 40th Street, New York, NY 10018. Phone: 1-800-221-2647.

KTeen Reg. US Pat. & TM Off.
Sunburst logo Reg. US Pat. & TM Off.

ISBN-13: 978-0-7582-6741-2
ISBN-10: 0-7582-6741-X

First Printing: May 2012
10 9 8 7 6 5 4 3 2 1

Printed in the United States of America

Creeping with the Enemy

Also by Kimberly Reid

My Own Worst Frenemy

No Place Safe

Published by Kensington Publishing Corporation

To James.

ACKNOWLEDGMENTS

Readers—thank you for sharing Chanti's world with me.

Chapter 1

The line in the Center Street bodega is five deep because it's Freebie Friday and the tamales are buy one, get one. I don't mind the wait—the scent of green chili reminds me how lucky I am to live on Aurora Avenue, just two blocks from the best tamales on the planet. Seeing how it's smack in the middle of Metro's second worst police zone, there isn't a lot to appreciate about the Ave, so that's saying something about these tamales.

Since they only let you get one order, I always find someone to go along who doesn't love them like I do so I can get one extra. Today my tamale pimp is Bethanie—we're numbers six and seven in line—and she's calling me some choice words for making her wait for a free tamale when she can afford to buy the whole bodega. I'm trying to explain to her that there's no sport in being rich (not that I would know) when a guy walks in from a Ralph Lauren ad and becomes number eight in line.

I don't know how a person could look so out of place and seem completely at ease at the same time, but this guy is pulling it off. He's also checking out Bethanie so hard that even though he's a complete stranger, he makes me feel like I'm the one who crashed the party.

"Did you lose something over here or what?" I ask the dude since Bethanie doesn't seem to mind him staring at us like we're on the menu with the tamales.

"Chanti, that's so rude," Bethanie tells me, never taking her eyes off Preppie. "Pay her no mind. She simply gets out of sorts when she's hungry."

First off, it's none of this complete stranger's business how I get when I'm hungry. It doesn't matter that he looks like a model, I pretty much don't trust anyone with my business. You never know how they might use it against you, even something as minor as your eating pattern. No, I'm not paranoid—I'm speaking truth. Second, why is she talking like that? *Pay her no mind. She simply gets out of sorts.* Bethanie's still working on her old money, rich girl impersonation, so maybe she thinks the girls Preppie hangs around talk that way.

"What's so good in here that people are willing to wait for it?" he asks Bethanie. He pretty much ignores me, so I almost laugh when his line goes right over her head.

"Supposedly the tamales are," she says, "but I've never had them."

I'm no pro at the flirty thing, but I'm sure he wasn't expecting her answer to be *tamales*. I move forward in the line, ignore their small talk and study the five-item menu as though I don't know what to order. Now there are only two people in front of me. Some Tejano music and the smell of cooking food drifts into the store from somewhere behind the clerk. I imagine somebody's grandmother back there wrapping corn husks around masa harina and pork. Yum.

I check out Preppie Dude like I'm not really looking at him but concentrating on the canned peaches on the shelf behind him. Cute. Not so cute he couldn't at least say hello to me before he starts fiening for my friend. He's still the last person in line even though tamale happy hour starts at four o'clock and the line is usually out the door until five. Weird, because it's only four thirty. I'm about to mention how weird that is to Bethanie, but she's finally figured out Preppie is flirting with her and has apparently forgotten me, too.

Now there's just one person ahead, Ada Crawford, who lives across the street from me and who I'm pretty sure is a prostitute even though I don't have any proof. If we lived in a different neighborhood, I might say she was a call girl since her clients come to her. But we live in Denver Heights, so she doesn't get a fancy title. Luckily, she hasn't noticed me behind her because I'm not supposed to be here and I wouldn't want her to tell my mother she saw me. Not that Ada ever has much to say to my mom.

Still no one else has come in. Even more strange is the fact there's only one person working the counter on busy Freebie Friday, a man I've never seen before and I'm a regular. Along with the new clerk, maybe they've also changed the cut-off time to four thirty. I suppose the owners would go broke if all people did was come in for the Freebie and not buy anything else. Or worse, get a friend to pimp an extra Freebie. I place my order—feeling slightly guilty—when I hear the bells over the door jangling a new arrival just as Ada walks away with her order. I look back to see a man holding the door open for Ada. He stays by the door once she's gone, and just stands there looking at the three of us still in line. He's jumpy. Nervous. He looks around the bodega but doesn't join the line and doesn't walk down the aisles of overpriced food. His left hand is in the pocket of his jacket.

My gut tells me to get out of the store. *Now.*

Just as I grab Bethanie's arm, the man brings his hand out of his jacket. It's too late.

"All right, everybody stay cool. Don't start none, won't be none. Just give me what's in the drawer," he says to the clerk, pointing the gun at him.

I'm hoping the clerk won't try to jump bad and pull out whatever he has under the counter. Every owner of a little mom-and-pop in my neighborhood has something under the counter. Or maybe it's in the back with the tamale-making grandmother. But no one comes from the back and the clerk isn't the owner. From what I can tell, it's his first day and he apparently doesn't care about the money or the shop, because he opens the cash drawer immediately. Bethanie pretends she's from money, but I know she's a lot more like me than she lets on. She knows what to do in a situation like this. Stay quiet and let it play out. We steal a quick glance at one another and I know I'm right. Either she's been through it before, or always expected it to happen one day.

I'm trying to stay calm by thinking ahead to when it will be over. Ninety seconds from now, this will just be a story for us to tell. The perp will be in his car taking the exit onto I-70. Hopefully I will not have puked all over myself by then. Or worse.

But then the cute guy speaks.

"Look man, just calm down."

What the hell? *Just shut up*, I want to scream. The clerk has already put the money into a paper bag and he's handing it over right now. This will all be over in thirty seconds if Preppie will just shut up.

The perp turns the gun in our direction. I lock eyes with him even though I know it's not the smartest thing to do. He realizes I can identify him; I can see him thinking about it, wondering what to do next. Suddenly, the smell of tamales sucker punches me and my stomach lurches. The wannabe-hero turns his back to the perp and shields Bethanie, pushing her to the ground and sending the contents of her bag all over the bodega floor. That move is like a cue for the perp. He breaks our gaze, grabs the paper bag from the clerk, and takes off.

I was right—it's over in just about ninety seconds. None of us wants to stick around to give the cops a statement. Preppie, who might have gotten us all killed, helps Bethanie grab the stuff that fell out of her bag while I scan the store for cameras. There aren't any that I can tell. As the three of us leave the store, the clerk is picking up the phone to call either the owner or the police, depending on how good the owner is about obeying employment laws and paying his taxes. I manage not to puke until I reach the parking lot.

"Clean yourself up and let's get out of here," Bethanie says, handing me a fast-food napkin from her purse to wipe my mouth. It smells like a fish sandwich and perfume, which doesn't do a thing for my upset stomach.

"But we're witnesses," I say, though I have no intention of sticking around, either. But saying it makes me feel like I at least considered doing the right thing.

"Exactly. Get in the car and open your window. I don't want my car smelling like sick."

I do what she says and tell myself I have to leave because Bethanie is my ride, even though I'm only two blocks from home. She hustled me out of the store and to her car because she's hiding something and has been since I met her a little over a month ago. So far, I've figured out that she lied her way into Langdon Preparatory School, pretending to be poor so she could get in on a scholarship because the only remaining slots were for the underprivileged. Like me. Unlike Bethanie, I never wanted to be there. Lana—that's my mother—forced me to because she was worried that I'd get into trouble in my neighborhood school.

That's the real reason I don't stay around to talk to the cops. The minute I tell her I can identify that perp, Lana will take me down to the police department to pick him out of a lineup. That would be a problem because one, I am a total wuss and don't want some pissed-off bad guy after me for retaliation. And two, Lana will put me on lockdown immediately following the lineup, just when I'm beginning to have a life.

This is one of the many drawbacks to having a cop for a

mother. She sees nothing but bad all day so she figures her number-one job is to shield me from it. That's a tough gig in our neighborhood, so she made me go way across town to this rich prep school, which turned out to have more bad guys than there are on my street. She made me quit working at the Tastee Treets because a couple of crackheads held it up one night during my shift. If she finds out about the robbery at the bodega, she'll make me identify the perp because she takes being a cop seriously, then she'll put me into her own version of a witness protection program because she takes being a mother seriously.

And I can't have that because, as I said, I am finally beginning to have a social life. It's sad to admit, but I am a high school junior who had never been kissed—I mean really kissed where you feel it in every part of you and you wonder how you were able to survive without it, as though oxygen and water and food will never be enough to sustain you ever again because of that kiss—until just two weeks ago. To my credit, I'm a year younger than the average junior, so the fact that I'm a late bloomer isn't all that weird. Now that I'm finally blooming, there is no way anyone can stop me from having that kind of kiss again.

Bethanie definitely won't tell anyone what happened today. That's a fact. She's been through something worse than what just went down. I know this not just because she didn't lose her lunch in the parking lot like I did, but because of something she said to me when I figured out she was really rich and she thought I might expose her: *You don't know nothing about me or where I come from. I can tell you now—I'm never going back.* She's running from something bad, and anytime someone's running, it's either from the cops or from someone who is being chased by the cops, which is probably worse.

I'm not sure why Preppie was in such a hurry to get out of here—maybe he doesn't want his friends to know he was slumming in Denver Heights—but he was gone by the time Bethanie and I got into her car.

I just hope the bodega didn't have a surveillance camera I missed when I made a quick scan of the store, that the clerk doesn't recognize me from the neighborhood (not a stretch since I've never seen him before), and that there were no witnesses who saw me go in or out. Then it would be as though I was never there. That's why I get into Bethanie's car even though I know it's wrong to run. I guess the owner minds all the laws because we can hear the sirens approaching as we drive away.

Chapter 2

When I walk into the house, Lana is peering through the miniblinds, dressed like she's going to the club. That means she's playing either a hooker or a drug dealer tonight. She works in the Vice Division, which investigates crimes related to prostitution, narcotics, and gambling and involves a lot of undercover work, so she almost never looks like a normal mother when she goes to work. Since people around here think she's a paralegal, Lana always wears a coat over her undercover clothes, even in the summer, which must make our neighbors think she's weird. Better than having them think she's a cop.

"Who was that driving a seven series BMW?" Lana is suspicious because the people on Aurora Avenue driving that kind of car are usually the people she's trying to arrest.

"A girl from school gave me a ride home."

I'm trying my best to stay cool because Lana has a special gift for reading people, especially liars, which is what makes her such a good cop. You mix that skill with the fact she knows me better than anyone and I'm basically an open book to her. Lucky for me, I'm an exceptional liar when I need to be, and sometimes I can even fool Lana.

"Her parents are brave letting a kid borrow a car nice as that."

"That's *her* car."

"Get outta here. A girl your age is driving a car that must cost as much as two of mine?"

"More like four of yours—when the guy you bought it from bought it *new*. That's the kind of school you forced on me—a place where kids drive cars that cost more than my mother makes in a year."

I've been at Langdon nearly two months and still haven't gotten used to needing ten minutes to get from one class to another because the ivy-covered campus is bigger than two city blocks and my classes are in three different buildings. After my old high school, it's taking more than a minute to get used to kids rolling up in Lexus SUVs instead of getting off the city bus (that would be me) and walking half a mile before even reaching Langdon Prep's quarter-mile-long drive-way. I'm used to people making weekend plans that include going to the movies or hanging at the mall. At Langdon, people talk about skiing in Aspen or flying to their winter home in the Virgin Islands. Lana and I have to make do with the same house all four seasons, and before Lana made detective and we lived on a beat cop's salary, there were some first-of-the-months we weren't sure we'd have even that. Yeah, I pretty much hate Langdon Prep.

"Hey, I gave you the chance to leave the school," Lana says, still looking out the window though Bethanie must have pulled away by now. "You wanted to stay."

She's right. I guess I can't keep playing the martyr thing. I stayed because of a boy. I know, totally cliché—but you haven't seen the boy. Marco is yum, and completely worth all the other stuff I hate about that school.

Lana finally turns away from the window and says, "Well, I'd rather see you roll up with an overindulged Langdon student than that ex-con down the street."

"I thought you were going to give MJ a break since she helped you solve a case. Oh yeah, and saved my *life*."

"I'm grateful to her for all the above, but I'd prefer you being friends with that preacher's daughter, or Tasha. What happened between you two, anyway? I hardly see her anymore."

MJ is what happened. When she and I started hanging out, I kinda neglected my friendship with Tasha, my BFF since third grade. As for the preacher's daughter—Michelle—we aren't really friends. Or even sort of. We tolerate each other because Tasha's friendship is the only thing we have in common. I'm guessing Michelle has even less love for me now, given my involvement in her sorry boyfriend's recent arrest. She ought to be grateful, but I doubt that's how she sees it.

Last semester I was arrested for running a home burglary ring, then the guy who was the *real* ringleader almost killed me and would have if MJ hadn't busted him to Lana. It hasn't been a month and Lana has already forgotten what she said when all that went down, which was how I could do worse for a friend. While it wasn't a glowing endorsement of MJ, it was better than what she's saying now. I'm about to ask why she'd think a rich friend would be better than one who would risk her own life to save me—like MJ did—when she looks at me funny.

"What's wrong with you, Chanti?"

"Nothing." Oh snap, here it comes. Supercop zeroing in on the target.

"Don't lie to me, girl."

"I don't know what you're talking about."

"You're sick. Your eyes are bloodshot, your color doesn't look right." She steps closer to me. "You *are* sick. Trying to cover it up with breath mints. Must be the flu."

"I'm not *that* sick, Mom."

"Oh, I see. You must have something planned this weekend if you're calling me 'Mom.' You won't be going anywhere but to bed, and get the thermometer from the medicine cabinet on your way. I'll be in there to read it, so don't try to fool me on the temperature."

I'm smiling all the way to my bedroom. What a lucky break. Lana's so sure she's busted me trying to hide the flu that it will never occur to her that I'm trying to cover up something entirely different. So I'll be on lockdown all weekend, but that's better than for the rest of my life, and that's exactly what would happen if Lana finds out about the bodega robbery and how I didn't help the cops or the store owner.

Not long after Lana left for work this morning to continue last night's stakeout, Bethanie called and asked if I wanted to hang. I had spent the last twenty-four hours waiting for the phone to ring, expecting some friend of Lana's from Robbery Division saying they had surveillance tape of her kid witnessing a holdup. I hadn't expected a call from Bethanie asking if I wanted to go to the mall, like what happened yesterday never did. We hadn't said a word while she drove me home right after the robbery, nothing except "See ya" when she pulled up in front of my house.

Now I felt guilty just talking to her, but I'd also been in bed pretending to be sick for the last twenty-four hours and really needed a diversion. Tasha started training for her new job at the movie theater this morning, so I can't call her. MJ and I still aren't on regular speaking terms. So I told Bethanie to come by and pick me up. When she gets here, I'll tell her Lana has me on lockdown with a fake cold and I can't go shopping. If I'd told her that on the phone, she probably wouldn't have come across town just to visit. Maybe it's the guilt of not staying around for the police report, or it could be having had a gun pulled on me by a meth addict, but yesterday has messed with my head. I really need to talk to someone about what happened and she's the only person who can know.

When I open my door, Bethanie doesn't even greet me, just asks if I have her phone.

"Why would I have your phone? And why did you keep your car running? That's not the best idea. You aren't in Cherry Creek anymore."

"It's okay, I'm not coming in. I had my phone when I went into the store to get your stupid free tamales. I went to use it after I dropped you at home yesterday and it was gone."

"It probably fell out of your bag with all your other stuff when Preppie tackled you to the floor."

"He didn't tackle me—he saved me. Anyway, that's what I figured so I checked the bodega."

"You went back there? We got out clean and now—"

"I'm not stupid, and I definitely don't need the police in my life. I waited an hour to make sure the cops were gone, then sent someone else inside to look."

"Who?"

"That's not important—my missing phone is. The person I sent checked on the floor under the shelves and couldn't find it anywhere, and the guy at the desk didn't have it."

"Well, neither do I."

She looks at me like she's not sure she believes me, then says, "Well, the guy at the desk wasn't the same one who was there at the holdup. Maybe the first cashier has it. I'll check the bodega again."

"How do you know it wasn't the same guy if you sent someone else?"

"I was there, I just didn't go inside. I peeked in the door."

"That might have been dangerous if the first guy had been there and recognized you. He could have called the cops and told them a witness had come back. He was probably at the police station giving a report, which is what we should have done."

"Like you're never going back in there for the free tamales."

"You went back less than two hours after the robbery. By next Friday, that guy will have forgotten what I look like. Besides, he and your phone may never be seen again if he has it."

"Why do you say that?" she asks, sounding a little frantic.

"I go to the bodega practically every day and I've never seen him before. If I get robbed my first day on the job, I'm never coming back."

"I hope you're wrong."

"What's your obsession with that phone, anyway? You freaked out when Ms. Reeves took it from you in class a few weeks ago. Now this. You may be scamming Langdon Prep, but I *know* you can just go buy another one. For that matter, you can probably afford to buy AT and T."

"A phone is like an extension of yourself."

"A phone is like a communication device."

"Look, if you don't have it . . ." she says, turning to leave.

"Wait. I thought you wanted to hang out. You could have asked if I had your phone when you called. Maybe you really just want to talk about what happened yesterday."

"No, I wanted to see your face when I asked about it. I know how you like to snoop. I wanted to know if you had it and whether you'd looked through it."

It's the first chilly day of fall, so I close the door behind me to keep the heat in and walk past her to sit on the top step of the porch. It's clear she isn't coming in, so maybe I can get her to talk out here while we inhale the fumes from her idling car.

"Puffing is illegal, you know."

"What?"

"Letting your car run like that. Police will ticket you."

"How do you know this stuff? Besides, in this neighborhood, I'm sure they have more serious crime to fight than me and my car. So you really don't have my phone?"

"I told you I didn't. You seriously thought you'd be able to tell if I was lying? There are people a whole lot more skilled than you who have tried and can't figure out when I'm lying." Mostly Lana, but there have been a few others. "What's so important in your phone that you think I'd not only snoop but then lie about snooping?"

"Nothing special. Same as what's in yours."

"Somehow I doubt it. I've just got a few numbers—hardly an extension of myself. Let me guess—the secret formula for the cure to acne? Compromising photos?"

She looks at me like I'm stupid until I mention the photos. Then she turns slightly red.

"Oh no, Bethanie. Please tell me you haven't been sexting photos of yourself. But if so, who to?"

"Don't be an idiot."

"Well, considering your concern about people snooping, you should put a password on it."

"I did. Okay, I *will* if I ever get it back."

"Since you're here, you want to watch a movie or something? My mother thinks I'm sick because I came home smelling like puke."

"Ew. Gross."

"Yeah, well, that's how I react to possibly getting shot. You know, like what happened yesterday?"

"We were nowhere close to getting shot, drama queen. Haven't you ever been in a holdup before?"

She says it like a normal person would say, "Haven't you ever been to Disneyland before?"

"Wow, you must have lived hard before that lottery ticket turned you into Paris Hilton."

"Stop snooping, Chanti."

"If you won't have a sharing moment, at least keep me company for a minute. Lana won't let me leave the house."

"Who?"

"My mom."

"You call her by her name? My mother would never play that."

"She was a little squeamish about being sixteen and having a kid, so when I started talking she taught me to call her Lana, thinking it almost sounds like *mama*," I explain. That's one answer. The other is that it's better if as few people as possible know Lana has a kid, considering her clientele are big on revenge.

"Well, just leave and get back before she does. How's she gonna know?"

"She has her ways."

If only my friends knew how good they have it with regular parents who don't surveil and interrogate liars for a living.

"I need to go find my phone," she says, even though she's still sitting next to me on the step. "Let me ask you—what did you think of that guy at the bodega? Hot, right?"

"So the only thing you want to discuss about what happened yesterday is the hot guy?"

"I told you we were never in any real danger. That methhead just wanted a few dollars for his next fix."

"Junkies are the most dangerous kind of thief. Besides, how would you know about that dude needing a fix, Cherry Creek girl?"

"You know by now I wasn't always Cherry Creek, so stop trying to game me."

Is she finally going to tell me what her deal is? I know she's rich, and that she got all her money from the lottery even though her parents are trying to pretend they got it from being in the oil business. I know she wants Langdon Prep to think she's poor until she can figure out a way to tell them she scammed her way into the school. I know she hasn't been in Colorado as long as she claims because her accent has plenty of South in it no matter how she tries to hide it. I found out all of this on my own. But what I haven't figured out is what she's hiding behind all those lies.

"Sure, if *you* stop gaming me. I know you weren't raised

here. Where are you really from? Texas, maybe?" I always figured Texas since she came up with that family oil story. We have a few drills around Colorado, but nothing like Texas.

"See, that's what I mean about you always trying to get in somebody's business."

We're quiet for a second, watching two little boys who have come up to admire her car.

"What about that guy, though?" she asks.

"He was cute." I don't add that he was the one who almost got us killed, trying to act all heroic just when the perp was about to leave the store.

"How about the way he protected me when the meth-head pointed his gun my way?"

"At us. He pointed it at *us,* but your hero only tried to save you."

"I know. Isn't that romantic? Too bad I never got his name."

Only Bethanie could recall a near-death experience and regret not getting some guy's number.

"Don't you feel bad about not sticking around to talk to the police?"

"Please. The cops never did anything for me."

"Not so much to help them, but to help the owner, and all the other owners that dude might rob next."

"Grow up, Chanti. We're all in this for ourselves. The bodega owner knows that. I know it. You're the only one who seems not to understand how it works. Living around here, I'd think you'd know. Those kids probably do," she says, pointing to the boys still checking out her car.

She's right about that. If they were old enough to see over the steering wheel and reach the gas pedal, I'd be concerned they were doing more than admiring the car. Even then, you never know if they might be casing it for someone old enough to drive. Bethanie must realize the same thing.

"I gotta bounce," she says as she gets up from the step. "See you in school Monday."

"Maybe. If I'm over my illness."

"I thought you weren't really sick."

"I wasn't, until now."

It was true. As I watch Bethanie drive away, I actually do feel sick—about running from the scene of a crime, about lying to Lana, but mostly about the uneasy feeling I get whenever Bethanie and I spend more than a few minutes together.

Chapter 3

Monday morning, Lana deems me well enough to go to school, which I expected because I was never really sick. I didn't miss Langdon, but I definitely missed Marco Ruiz. He's the one who gave me the kiss that I'm sure I could subsist on forever . . . well, along with water and Reese's cups. But I wouldn't know because we haven't kissed again since that first time. It happened in the days right after the burglary ringleader almost killed me. He almost killed Marco, too, so his mother has forbidden him to date me, even before we've gone out on a single real date. Something about how I'm a menace to her son's well-being and leading him down a dangerous path. Blah, blah. She even called my mom and got her in on the plan. Lana says I'm a catch for any guy, but I have to respect his parents' wishes. It doesn't matter that I saved Marco from jail and worse. I suppose Mommie Dearest could say he wouldn't have been in trouble if he didn't know me, and she'd have a point.

The thing I won't admit to anyone is that I'm kind of glad Mrs. Ruiz doesn't like me and wants to keep me away from Marco. Before we kissed, I must have imagined it happening a thousand times, and when we finally did, it was pretty much perfect. So I'm not averse to it happening again.

The problem is what comes after. If Marco and I go where Mrs. Ruiz doesn't want us to go, he'd be my first real boyfriend. Outside of a couple of bad dates, I'm a complete amateur when it comes to boys. Being younger than all the kids in my class does nothing for my confidence, either. Marco's seventeen and I'm not even sixteen yet. I bet his old girlfriend isn't the complete noob I am. What if he compares me to her? Unless he needs her to solve a case for him, I'm sure I'd lose that contest.

Fortunately, Marco's the kind of guy who respects his parents *and* their wishes. I know—I picked the one guy on the planet who actually stays away from what his parents forbid instead of running to it like smelly freshmen boys run to a bottle of Axe body spray after PE. But he's still a guy, and even if he won't officially date me, he tries everything else he can in the limited time and space we have together. He's thinking I'll eventually win his mother over and we can pick up where we left off a few weeks ago with that kiss in the library. I'm hoping by the time his mother changes her mind, I'll have a clue what *pick up where we left off* actually means.

For now, I have an excuse not to get too close. Marco and I used to work together at a moving company, but we both quit that job since we didn't get along so well with the owner's kids. Mostly we just text and talk on the phone, which he figures is not the same as dating me, and his parents specifically said no *dating*. They didn't say anything about no communicating. I give good talk and text because they're done at a distance and perfectly safe. But what to do when he wants more? Worse—I imagine all this almost-dating is creating anticipation on his part that I absolutely won't be able to manage when and if Mrs. Ruiz decides she loves me.

I even catch a break at school. Marco and I have a couple of classes together and share one-minute conversations in the hall between bells, but nothing more than that because the hallways have eyes—namely those of Headmistress Smythe.

She's had it in for me since I started Langdon, so she has no problem honoring Mrs. Ruiz's request to keep an eye on Marco and me to make sure we don't get together. I figure it's only a matter of time before I somehow win Mrs. Ruiz's heart, get over my first-boyfriend jitters, improve my woefully inadequate skills of seduction, and take Marco down that path of sin his mother is so worried about. If only she knew I'd need a GPS, a map, and a tour guide just to *find* the path, much less navigate it.

"How was your weekend?" I ask when I find him at his locker.

"All right. Better when I was thinking of you."

Oh man, does he know what to say. I wish I did.

"Any change on the home front?" I ask, keeping up the charade that I'm as eager as he is to move beyond hallway dates.

"Not yet. But she'll come around. Just give it some time, okay?"

He puts his hands around my waist and looks at me that way he does and I forget about everyone around us and even how nervous the whole boyfriend thing makes me . . . until I hear my name—my full name—being yelled at me from across the hall, in a completely fake British accent.

"Chantal Evans! In my office, now."

Where did *she* come from? I swear, I need to put a bell on her.

"Headmistress Smythe, wait—I'm as much to blame," Marco says in my defense.

"Oh, I doubt that. Get to class, Mr. Ruiz. Miss Evans, come with me."

I follow her, wondering what story I might give to keep her from calling Lana. Oh yeah. She won't be calling Lana because Smythe thinks my mother is in jail doing time. For what, I don't know. All I've been able to figure out is that Lana was able to get me accepted into Langdon by calling in a favor, and the favor has something to do with Smythe. Which means Smythe had something to do with a crime that occurred while Lana was undercover as whatever criminal Smythe thinks she is. Of course Lana won't give me the dirt, not that I haven't tried to get it out of her. Having that kind of information could make my life at Langdon so much easier.

"Chantal, can't you stay out of trouble for more than a week?"

"Headmistress Smythe, with all due respect, I really haven't been in trouble for at least two weeks. Besides, I solved those school thefts and got the real thieves arrested, didn't I?"

"Well, yes."

I can tell that admission was as painful as if I'd asked her to admit that she really isn't British, her hair really isn't auburn, and that she really did something illegal enough to make her owe Lana a favor.

I try to reason with her. "This thing going on between Marco and his parents—it's just a classic misunderstanding, like the Capulets and the Montagues in *Romeo and Juliet,* except one-sided."

"And we know how that turns out, don't we?" she says.

I could stand there and argue with old Smythe because I like a good debate, but I hate confrontation. There's a fine line between the two and I don't plan on crossing it. At least now I get to see Marco a little bit. If I push too hard, his mom might send him back to North High and far away from me.

"You're right, Mrs. Smythe. Marco and I will do what his parents want."

"I'm glad you're being sensible."

That's me, sensible. That's all I ever am, but it still doesn't seem to keep me out of trouble.

After school, Bethanie is hanging out with me near the gym entrance where I hope to catch Marco on his way to football practice. I got a message from him last period that maybe we could hang out for a few minutes between last bell and the start of practice. When I tried to text back, the teacher caught me and took my phone until the end of class. So I couldn't answer until a few minutes ago, but I haven't heard back from him. I feel a little like a groupie, but I don't care. As pathetic as my love situation is, Bethanie's is worse, which is why she's willing to wait with me until he shows, if he shows. I think she's living vicariously through the barely there relationship Marco and I have. Or through *Romeo and Juliet,* which we're currently reading in English Lit. Now *that* story is tragic, and makes pathetic look not so bad.

"I thought you already finished that," I say when Bethanie pulls Shakespeare out of her backpack and starts reading.

"It's so good, I'm reading it again. Can you imagine having a love like they had?"

"Their whole forbidden love thing is definitely familiar. I just hope my story turns out better than theirs did."

"I'm telling you," she is saying, "the minute you give it up, he'll forget what his parents look like, much less obey their rule about not dating you. That's how guys are once you put it on them. They can't think straight, and *you* make the rules, not Mommy."

"You've been misinformed. Once you give it up, they forget your number and move on to the next target," I say, thinking of some girls I know on the Ave.

"So ignore me. I'm not the one crying into her pillow every night."

"I have not cried even *once* into my pillow. When Marco and I do it, *if* we ever do it, I want it to be because we both want to, not because I'm trying to manipulate him."

"So all the other women before us who have been using it as collateral, for like—centuries—had it wrong? I don't think so."

"You might be right, but I won't play it like that."

"Yeah, well, you won't be playing at all, at least not with Marco, if all y'all do is meet for thirty seconds at your locker every day. A boy that hot will find other means."

Bethanie doesn't know how right she is. If Marco and I ever get together for real, I could be joining the ranks of those girls on the Ave. This year my old high school merged with North High, where Marco used to go and where I'd be going, along with Michelle and Tasha, if I hadn't gotten the scholarship to Langdon. According to Tasha—whose gossip is usually dead-on, as much as I hate to admit it—Marco was something of a player at North.

But he wasn't like your average player running games and telling a girl's business all over school. The way Tasha heard it, he was still the same sweet guy I know, mindful of his parents, respectful to teachers, and always a gentleman with girls. He was so sweet, in fact, girls everywhere were willing to drop the panties for him. And like I said, no matter how sweet Marco is, he's still a guy. So you can see why I'm a little intimidated. Between his rep and my rookie status, the score stands at Chanti—*one,* Marco's ex-girlfriend—*infinity.*

Just then, the *boy that hot* steps out of the gym door, fully dressed in his football gear.

"Hey, I just saw your text," Marco says.

"Ms. Hemphill caught me and took my phone. I couldn't send an answer until the end of school."

"Aw, man, I didn't get to spend any time with you," he says, stepping closer to me until he notices Bethanie staring at us.

"Bethanie, don't you have to be somewhere?" I say.

"Nope."

I could knock her out. The deal was she'd hang with me until Marco showed. The least she could do is keep reading Shakespeare instead of gawking at us. Just then, a bunch of players comes through the gym doors behind Marco.

"Maybe tomorrow," Marco says, trailing his fingers down

my arm, grabbing my hand and holding it for just a second before he leaves to join his team. I watch him jog toward the practice field until he's hidden behind the gym. I want him; I want him not. No, I really do want him, I just don't know what to do with him.

As we head for the front of Langdon and the long drive-way—Bethanie to her secret parking spot, me to the bus stop—she says, "You do know how sad this is, right?"

I'm about to ask how she knows so much about men since in the time I've known her, she's never mentioned a boyfriend past or present and she's a whole year older than I am, when we see a guy leaning against the railing of the stairs that lead from the drop-off circle at the top of the driveway to the main entrance. We can't help but notice him. Not only is he gorgeous and not wearing the Langdon uniform, but he has this style about him that lets you know right off he isn't a Langdon boy, like he's older. He's probably in college, maybe even a junior or senior, and looks totally out of place at Lang-don even though he's wearing all the preppie gear. It's the guy from the bodega robbery, the one who almost got us killed. I had an uneasy feeling about him then that I couldn't place. It just got a lot stronger.

When he spots us, he smiles and starts moving in our di-rection.

"Chanti, that's the guy," Bethanie whispers. If she weren't trying to play it cool, she'd be squealing.

"You've been talking to this guy?"

"No, but I've been dreaming about talking to him, all the things I'd say if I ever got the chance."

"Let's pretend we didn't see him and go inside Main Hall."

"You must be kidding," she says, heading straight toward him.

I look around and see that there are plenty of people still hanging out waiting for rides home, plus a group of teachers talking just a few feet away. I know I get a little paranoid, but I can't help it. I mean, how did this guy even know where to find Bethanie?

"Hi—it's Bethanie, isn't it?" he says when he reaches us.

"She goes by Beth," I say, just to establish from the start that I'm standing right here. Back at the bodega, I don't think dude even knew I was there.

She rolls her eyes at me and says, "I go by *Bethanie*. With an *ie*. You're the guy from the store, right?"

As if she didn't know.

"I'm Cole." He reaches into his pocket and I'm ready to duck, but he only pulls out Bethanie's phone. I'd recognize it anywhere since it's all blinged out in cubic zirconia, although knowing Bethanie, they're probably real diamonds. I bet that's the reason she guards that phone with her life. "You dropped this at the store that day. You were already gone when I noticed it on the floor."

"Didn't you leave the store when we did?" I ask. It isn't really a question, because I know for a fact he had driven away before Bethanie could get her key in the ignition.

"I've been looking everywhere for that," Bethanie says.

They're ignoring me, just like at the bodega.

"I'm sorry to stake out your school like this, but I didn't know how else to reach you."

Uh-huh. At least he knows his game is a little stalkerish.

"How did you know to find her at Langdon?" I ask.

He looks me dead in the eye and smiles, but says to Bethanie, "You've got a good friend here. She looks out for you."

"Well?" I say.

More eye rolling from Bethanie.

"I hope you don't mind, but I did scroll through a couple of your texts and saw Langdon Prep mentioned a couple of times."

"Bethanie, you really should lock your phone. You never

know who might find it." I cross my arms all defiant-like, for-getting that I'm a wuss, because I become momentarily brave when I get my girl detective on. "What did you say your last name was again?"

"He didn't. You have to excuse her—she's had no home training," Bethanie says, taking the phone from Cole and turning it on. I try to catch a look over her shoulder and see she's scrolling through her photo album. Seems like she'd check her messages first thing. Whatever it is, she looks satis-fied and puts it in her bag.

Cole is standing there like he's waiting for something.

"Were you expecting a reward?" I ask.

"Chanti, don't you have somewhere to be?" Bethanie asks.

"Nope."

"Chanti and I were just about to go inside to get a Coke from the soda machine. Do you want something to drink?"

I'm pretty sure a guy who tracks a girl down the way Cole did is looking for more than liquid refreshment, but I'm not sure what it is. Somehow I don't think it's just a guy lust-ing for a girl. Something about Cole feels off. Forced maybe. The way he showed up at the bodega—looking like he'd never step foot in a bodega—on the day it gets robbed. The way he happened to find her phone even though he left the store before we did. Makes me think he took it when every-thing fell out of Bethanie's bag just so he could find her to re-turn it. Just in case he's considering her offer to get a soda, I give him the evil eye. He looks at me and gives the slightest hint of a smile.

"I'd better get going," Cole says. "Just wanted to make sure you had your phone."

My evil eye is scarier than I think, or he knows I'm suspi-cious. Either way, he turns to leave. Bethanie takes a step to-ward him and for a second, I'm worried she's going to follow him.

"Come on, Bethanie. I really need that soda," I say, pulling her arm. I'm thinking it's a good idea if we go inside for a few minutes. My paranoia may be in overdrive and Cole may be just a considerate guy, but I prefer he'd not know about Bethanie's secret parking space or my long walk to the bus stop.

"It was really nice of you to find me, Cole," Bethanie says, but he's too far away to hear her.

Chapter 4

Every sentence Bethanie speaks now starts or ends with *Cole*. At first, her conversations were made up of things she imagined about him, like which college he probably attended, whether or not he had a job (she decided he did not, but was independently wealthy like her), and that he had been unlucky in love because he hadn't found the right girl (she decided the right girl would be her). When he wasn't busy counting his money or pining for her, Bethanie had also decided Cole volunteered at the homeless shelter, donated to the Humane Society, and helped little old ladies cross Broadway during rush hour. After a couple of days of her imagination gone wild, I could tell that she was no longer imagining he was a god; he had actually *done* something that made her think he was.

"Cole doesn't believe in fast food," she's saying in response to my request that we stop for a two-piece-with-biscuit before she drops me at home.

"It's Popeyes, not a religion," I say, though I realize that it almost is. When I'm really hungry and it smells like they just fried a fresh batch, I'd be willing to kneel at the counter and say the Lord's Prayer just to get a wing.

"He's really into the locally based sustainable slow-food movement."

"The what?"

I'm getting irritated because I already called Tasha and told her I'd bring something home for her and Michelle since I'm always inviting myself to their moms' cooking, and Bethanie really needs to get into the right lane now if we're going to Popeyes.

"You know what that is," she says as though I'd asked her what chocolate is.

"I really don't. And why would I want someone to serve my food slowly? Uh, you should be changing lanes now. It's coming up soon."

"The food isn't served slowly. Cole says food grown or raised within a few miles of where it's eaten, produced without chemicals and steroids, is better for us and for the environment."

"Well, unless Cole is nearby with a crispy free-range chicken and a hot, buttery biscuit, I really wish you'd get over now because I'm hungry and Popeyes is at the next light."

"When aren't you hungry? Whatever. It's your body. Put crap in there if you want to."

Once I have my order, the box warm in my lap and the scent promising all kinds of goodness, I can relax and find out why her talk has gone from abstract fantasy to concrete platitudes about how I should eat.

"So you learned about Cole's food philosophy during the holdup?"

"Of course not. He was busy trying to protect me from dying."

"I thought you said we were never in any danger."

"Only because he was there to protect me," Bethanie says as she switches lanes, cutting off a delivery truck. "You're really going to make me wish I hadn't offered you a ride home, especially since I have to take you across town."

"We both know you only offered the ride so you could talk to me about Cole. You should be glad I'm so interested."

"Interested? More like interrogative."

"So when did he give you his food theory? He didn't mention it when he brought your phone."

"Okay, so he called me."

"You've been seeing this guy? You don't know anything about him."

"That's why they call it dating. When you first meet a guy, aka the Stranger, you don't know anything about him. You go on dates and learn things about him, which makes him no longer a stranger."

"You're *dating*?" I'm so disturbed by this that I have to open the box and pinch off a piece of biscuit for comfort.

"Not yet, but it's like we are. We talk on the phone for hours every night."

"You mean for the last two nights. It's Wednesday and you met him Monday."

"Really we met last Friday."

"During a holdup. I don't think that counts as a formal introduction."

"He asked me out this weekend."

"Are you crazy? Does he have a last name yet? How old is he, anyway?"

"He's twenty. I'll be seventeen in two weeks. It isn't a big deal at all."

"Well, until you *are* seventeen, it's statutory, which *is* a big deal."

"Oh my God, Chanti. I haven't even *seen* the guy since Monday. Now you've got us having sex and calling it . . . *that*? It would not be . . . *that* . . . even if we did get that far."

"That's exactly what it would be. You're a minor, he's an adult," I say like I know what I'm talking about when actually I don't. Living with a cop, I've learned a lot about the law, but this particular statute has never come up and I wouldn't dare ask Lana or she'd think it was me looking to score with an older man.

"Where do you get this stuff, Chanti?"

I realize I need to back off a little with the cop-speak. Especially while Bethanie is driving, because it's not like she's going to win any Motorist of the Year awards or anything, even without being upset.

"So I guess you told him yes to the date."

"Look, if you're that worried, come with us."

"Like a chaperone? I'm not that desperate for something to do."

"No, like a double date. And I think you are that desperate."

"Who would I get on such short notice?"

Bethanie gives me a pitiful and knowing look. "Hello? Marco."

"But he's off-limits," I say, hoping she'll convince me to talk him into it.

"Most kids' parents tell them not to see each other and they can't do anything but plot ways to see each other. You and Marco just roll over and play dead."

"Most kids don't have Lana for a mother."

"How's she so different? What's she going to do if you get caught—throw you in jail?"

Pretty much.

"I think it's sweet that Marco honors his parents," I say.

"Sweet won't get you out of the house this Saturday night, will it? Just tell him the truth—you're worried about me dating Cole. He already knows you're like an Olympic worrier. Tell him you'll just feel better if you can get to know the guy. If Marco is sweet as you say, he'll want to look out for me. If you get caught, y'all tell your parents it was for a good cause."

When Bethanie drops me off in front of Tasha's house, Tasha and Michelle are just coming up the sidewalk.

"Y'all must have been on the late bus," I say, trying to head off the conversation from where I know it will probably go.

"We had a Spanish Club meeting after school. Your friend too good to meet us, or what?" Tasha asks, watching Bethanie drive off. "She never sticks around when she brings you home."

"Stick around? She barely slows down to let Chanti out of the car," Michelle says. "That's how rich folks are—always scared not-rich people are looking to jack them."

"Or worried our condition might be catching," Tasha says. "Is everybody at your new school like that?"

If only they knew Bethanie is more ghetto-fabulous than any of us.

"Here's your food. Better eat while it's hot," I say, hoping to get them off the subject of my rude rich friend and onto another one.

Tasha grabs the bag from me, opens it, inhales the perfume of grease and chicken, and starts up her porch steps. "Thanks, Chanti. I needed this. You coming in to eat with us?"

"No, I'd better get started on my homework, but I did want to ask you if I missed any gossip."

That stops Tasha in her tracks because my girl loves gossip and always knows what's happening on the Ave.

"Ooh, like what?" Michelle asks, her voice starting to climb octaves like it does whenever she gets excited, which is why we sometimes call her Squeak.

"I don't have any gossip. That's why I'm asking y'all. I was at the bus stop this morning and thought I heard somebody talking about a robbery somewhere on Center Street last weekend."

"Somebody's always getting robbed on Center," Tasha says, looking a lot less interested in talking to me. "My two-piece is getting cold."

★   ★   ★

I'm at the kitchen table working on calculus equations, finally chill about the robbery because if Tasha doesn't know anything about it, no one on Aurora Ave. does. Lana is concocting something on the stove even though I told her I'd already eaten. She doesn't have a stakeout tonight, which is rare lately, so I'm glad we can hang out. I don't know if it's because we're pretty close in age as parents go, but I actually get along with my mother, for the most part. Even when we're working each other's last nerve, it's nothing like how my friends describe their relationships with their mothers, which, in some cases, sounds close to hell. The only bad thing about Lana being home at night is that she always cooks, and this truly is a bad thing. She cannot cook to save her life, which is why I'm always mooching dinner from Tasha and Michelle.

Whatever Lana's cooking smells like, I'm pretty sure what it will taste like: a blend of flavors that should never come together in the same pot. She'll watch cooking shows on Food Network, but instead of following the exact recipe, she'll add and subtract stuff to give it her "special touch." By the time she's done, the finished product has maybe two ingredients left from the original recipe, and it's almost always bad. I'm a little scared, because I swear I smell hot sauce and peanut butter, but I just keep doing my math homework and pray dinner will at least be edible.

"Did you hear about the bodega?" Lana asks. My stress-free mood has lasted all of two hours.

"No," I say, not really lying because I haven't *heard* anything about it. Hearing about something and actually witnessing it is not the same thing. "What about it?"

"I heard they got held up again."

"From someone at work?" I'm still waiting for some detective friend of hers to bust me for being at the bodega.

"No, from Ada Crawford."

"Ada?" Since when do Ada and Lana ever talk to each other?

"She was in there just before it happened. She got outside the bodega and realized the cashier had left out part of her order and was about to go back inside when she saw a man holding a gun on him."

"How did she see anything without going back inside? They've got so many beer posters and cigarette ads covering the glass, you can barely see anything inside or out."

"I guess the doors aren't completely covered up."

"Did she report it?"

"You know Ada tries to keep a low profile when it comes to the police, but at least she called them. Anonymously, of course. And since I'm supposed to be her neighbor the paralegal and not a cop, I can't really report anything she told me without blowing my cover."

So it wasn't the cashier who called the cops.

"It was just the cashier there when the police arrived on scene, no customers?" I ask.

"Maybe we ought to assign the investigation to you," Lana says, adding ketchup to her boiling cauldron.

"I'm just interested in what goes on in my neighborhood, that's all."

"Ada said there were two or three other people in there; some kids, she thought, but wasn't sure. They were positioned where she couldn't get a good look, but that's why she called 9-1-1. She was worried about the customers. I called a friend in Robbery to get some information, but they didn't have any. The witnesses Ada saw must have left before patrol arrived."

"How about the cashier? He must have reported something."

"That's the weird thing. When the uniforms arrived, the store was empty—no perp, no customers, no cashier. Even he left the scene. All the officers found was an unmanned store and no signs of foul play."

"Maybe Ada made it all up," I suggest.

"There is no way Ada Crawford is calling the police unless she has a very good reason. Most likely the cashier was in on the holdup, although they found money in the register."

That would explain why I'd never seen the cashier before. And I guess there wasn't a grandmother in the back making tamales after all, or she'd have been a witness. But I know for sure I saw the cashier put money in a paper bag and hand it to the robber. Maybe he didn't give it all away, which would make him the dumbest cashier ever because that's the quickest way to piss off a robber—holding out on him. My first time witnessing a holdup and it's the strangest one I've ever heard of. Now it sounds more like a phantom robbery. But at least now I don't have to worry about being called as a witness or having Lana find out I was in the bodega after she told me it was off-limits.

"This neighborhood is getting so bad I'm afraid to leave you here alone at night anymore."

"It's kind of hard to work vice and not work nights, Lana. Not a whole lot of vice going down at nine in the morning."

"I know, but Burglary wasn't so bad."

"Only because you love being a cop, so you'd rather work in any department than not be one. But you love being a vice cop even more than just being a cop. I'm fine at night, really."

"Maybe we should get a dog. Better yet, it might be time for me to take you to the firing range."

"The dog is a better idea. I already know how to handle a gun."

"You're old enough to know more than how to handle it. I want you to know how to *use* it."

On summer trips to Atlanta, my grandfather would take me out to our cousin's farm in the country so we could shoot aluminum cans off a tree trunk. I know how to load, clean, and shoot a gun, but only the mechanics. She's talking about something entirely different now—the mental part. The part that involves confrontation and freaks me out completely.

That whole situation last semester that might cost me my relationship with Marco? It ended with me holding a gun on a bad guy. Later, I told Lana that I may have looked like I was in control, but I was pretty sure I couldn't have used the gun if I really had to. She always said you should never pick up a weapon of any kind unless you intended to use it. Otherwise the bad guy was certain to take it from you and have no hesitation about using it. I don't know if I'm ready for the firing range just yet. That's the real deal, complete with targets that look like people, even if they're only paper people. I don't want to talk about target practice and guns anymore, but I also don't want her to talk about the bodega, either.

"I don't know if I'm ready for the range yet."

"You attract trouble even though I try to keep you as far away from it as I can. Maybe instead of shielding you from trouble, I should be teaching you how to handle it if it comes."

"I'm fine, Lana, I swear."

"We could move . . ."

This is where the conversation always goes, which scares me almost as much as the talk about the firing range. Or whatever is simmering in that pot on the stove. It ain't much, but I love our house, the Ave, and the people on the street. At least the ones who haven't done time. Well, except for MJ Cooper, but she's going straight. By now, I know exactly what to say at this point in the conversation.

"This house is almost fully paid, which is no small thing living on one salary, a cop's salary, at that. And you know that house on the corner has had the FOR SALE sign in the yard so long it's faded."

"Because people are afraid to live here."

"But like you always say, what happened in North Highland is going to happen here—young couples with good tech and medical jobs are going to want to move to Denver Heights and put up Starbucks and tea shops and then we can sell for large dollars."

"That's true," she says, then turns from the stove to look at me. "You haven't been going to that bodega, have you?"

I try to judge whether she knows something and is just testing me. If she knows and I lie, I'm dead. If she doesn't know and I confess, I'm dead.

"You told me to stay away from there, right?"

"No one got hurt, thank goodness," she says, and turns back to the stove, satisfied with my pseudo-answer. See how I'm good at lying without lying? It's a gift, really.

"Didn't they have surveillance tape in there?" I ask, to close out my final worry.

"No—can you believe it? Who doesn't have cameras nowadays? Especially around here."

Suddenly, I feel so much relief. I guess I didn't realize how tense I was carrying around that lie-by-omission. I think I've averted any other bodega questions, but I'm glad for the phone ringing at that moment, just in case.

"Are you screening?" I ask Lana before I pick up.

"Yeah, and dinner's almost ready. I can't wait for you to try this new recipe I came up with."

I check the caller ID. "It's an Atlanta number, and not one I recognize. You think Papa got a new number?"

"No," Lana says, sounding almost angry. "Don't answer. If it's anyone worth talking to, they'll leave a message."

All of a sudden, I feel tension between Lana and me and I'm not sure why. Neither of us says anything for a minute, then Lana walks over to the phone base, puts it on speaker, and dials a number. The mechanical voice of the messaging system announces we have no new messages.

She turns to me, looking as relieved as I did a few minutes ago when I learned there was no surveillance tape at the bodega, and says, "See? I was right—no one important."

I'm not sure what all that was about, but I know better than to do anything but nod in agreement.

Chapter 5

It's Saturday night and now I find myself grateful for Bethanie's bodega hero-turned-stalker-turned-date. Marco was much easier than I expected to convince that we needed to check out Bethanie's new boyfriend, and not just because he's a good guy that way. I think all those hallway dates of ours are making him want more than that, no matter his mom's rules. All I've thought about for the last two months is this moment, but now that it's here, I'm a little nervous. I never thought our first real date would be with another couple, but I take what I can get. And what I get is perfect. Marco looks delicious when Bethanie and I find him waiting outside the restaurant. He's in a suit (how many times does a girl get to see her guy in a suit?) and while I'd love him in anything, this look is truly working for him. We're all dressed like something out of Oscar night because Cole picked a restaurant that no high school kid could afford unless it's a Langdon kid, and not one who is there only because they got a scholarship. I guess we know which couple will be picking up the tab.

I talked Bethanie into us driving together and letting the guys meet us there. Until I figure out what Cole is about, I'd rather her not be in a car alone with him. And if I was being honest, I'd admit the same thing about Marco and me, but for a different reason. Despite what Bethanie says, Cole's not some regular stranger—there's nothing regular about how he stalked her, and the more I replay the holdup, the more I think something was off about it. I mean *off* beyond the fact that it was a holdup and we were threatened at gunpoint.

Cole shows up right behind us in a tailor-made suit that looks like it costs ten of Marco's. His whole look is effortless, like he's used to the stiff collar and the tie. I'm pretty sure Marco is wearing his father's clothes, because the suit's a little tight (there's a reason Marco is the starting quarterback—muscle in all the right places). Unlike Mr. Smooth standing next to him, Marco keeps sticking his finger between his collar and neck, and is beginning to look a little uncomfortable. But that's okay because he'll still be the finest guy in the place.

While I'm trying to figure out what kind of job a twenty-year-old must have to afford to dress all *GQ* and know restaurants like this even exist—expensive and sustainably grown, of course—Cole is opening the door for all of us and acting like he's running the show. Marco definitely would have opened the door for us if he'd gotten to it first. If you were only going by his face, Cole looks our age but he still gets respect from the maître d', who leads us to a great table. Maybe that's what confidence and a good suit will do for you. I'm pretty sure the maître d' would have kicked the rest of us out of the place—Marco in his father's off-the-rack suit; me in a too-little black dress borrowed from Lana, who is a size smaller; and Bethanie in a tight, hot-pink sparkly dress that proves her tastes haven't yet caught up with her money. Yeah, without Cole, that maître d' would have kicked us out *and* called the police—or Tim Gunn—for extra measure.

When the hostess shows us our table, Marco guides me to my chair with his hand on the small of my back, and I just about faint. When he helps me slide my chair in, just like the leading man always does in the movies, he leans in close and whispers, "You look great, and smell even better." Does he have any idea how hard he's making it to focus on why I'm here?

By the time the appetizers arrive, I've calmed down enough to remember I have a job to do. Barely.

"So what do you do, Cole?" I ask.

"That's an odd question," he says.

"It seems pretty normal to me."

"For a thirty-year-old, maybe. Juniors in high school don't usually ask that."

"Once you get to know Chanti, you'll see that's just how she is, like a little old lady," Bethanie says. "She makes thirty seem young."

"Thirty *is* young," Cole says, sounding like Lana when I call someone her age old—a little defensive.

"Well, if you were also a junior in high school, I wouldn't have to ask. But Bethanie says you're twenty. Unless you were kept back *a lot,* I'm guessing you're done with summer reading lists and prepping for the SATs."

"No, I'm actually twenty-one, and no more SATs for me. I graduated college a few months ago, and for now, I'm just keeping my options open."

"Oh yeah?" Marco says. "Where'd you go to school?"

I give Bethanie the biggest stare-down possible and don't care if anyone notices. Did he just say twenty-one? I can imagine Bethanie explaining how five years is not a big deal. Twenty-one and twenty-six would be no big deal, but twenty-one and sixteen? I'm sorry, that's a problem. And probably a crime.

"Marco is seventeen, the same age I'll be in just a couple of weeks—a consenting party in the state of Colorado. I looked it up," Bethanie says, without giving Cole a chance to answer Marco's question and apparently reading my mind.

Cole looks slightly unnerved by Bethanie's announcement to the whole table that at some point, she plans on consenting to something, and I'm sure none of us think she meant just a second date. It's a strange reaction if you ask me. He should be glad she's looked up the law and found out he won't be breaking one. I mean—he *is* trying to hook up with her, right? Bethanie doesn't seem to notice how uncomfortable she's made her date—on their *first* date—and keeps right on talking.

"And Chanti's almost sixteen. Now that we have our ages out of the way, maybe we could talk about something more interesting."

"You're only fifteen? Impressive. You must be some kind of brainiac," Cole says to me, clearly trying to move the subject away from Bethanie and all her talk about the age of consent.

"My girl is mad smart," Marco says, leaning back a little and putting his arm on the back of my chair. My pre-boyfriend self would have called "macho ownership" on that move. My post-boyfriend self thinks it's the sweetest thing. Yep, I'm turning into *that* girl and I kinda like it.

"I skipped second grade."

"Second grade . . . I think that's a critical grade in the development of social skills," Bethanie says.

I take the hint and promise myself I'll be good at least until the main course. Besides, there's plenty to learn about a person just through observation. Like his accent. I love trying to figure out where a person is from based on their inflection, which is kind of hard since I haven't traveled much. But whenever I meet someone with an accent from somewhere other than Colorado, I try to learn where they're from. According to Bethanie, Cole's from DC, but as I listen to him wax on about slow food, I hear a lot more South in his voice than Washington, which claims to be Southern but really isn't. That *is* one of the few places I've traveled to, and it ain't the South no matter what the map says.

Since Cole is still talking about eating food grown locally, I see an opening.

"Speaking of locations, Bethanie tells me you're from DC, Cole. I have family in Atlanta so I go down there often. You sound a lot like someone from there."

"You have a really keen ear. Smart and observant—that could be dangerous," he says before flashing that con-artist smile of his to everyone at the table. "I guess I didn't explain that very well to Bethanie. I went to school in DC but grew up in a small town an hour outside Atlanta. I thought I'd lost the twang since I haven't been down there in a long time, but I guess some people can still detect the accent."

Bethanie looks at Cole like she's surprised, but he doesn't notice. I wish I knew what that look meant. If I had to guess, she either realizes he lied to her or he's lying to me, because she understood exactly what he said when he told her he was from DC. Or finding out he's from the South like she is— even though I haven't gotten her to tell me exactly where's she's from—has thrown her a little.

"I'm thinking about going to school in DC," Marco says, revealing something he's never told me. "Georgetown or American University. They have good poli-sci programs."

Huh? He told me he wants to go to college for engineering. I sneak a look at him and he smiles like he's up to something, like we have a secret. Oh, now I get it. He's trying to help me interrogate Cole. Is he not the greatest?

"That's what I hear," is all Cole says. I guess he doesn't plan on telling us anything about his college days, so I try another approach.

"What brings you to Denver, Cole?"

"There's that thing again where you talk like somebody's mother," Bethanie says, followed by a smile full of threat.

"It's okay, Bethanie," Cole says. "Who doesn't like talking about themselves?"

Bethanie doesn't, at least not the truth about herself.

"After school, I came out for a job opportunity. It didn't work out, but I like Denver so much, I decided to stay."

"And do what?"

"I'm still working on that, but I have some good leads."

"In the meantime, you're living off wealthy parents, a trust fund, or what?"

"Chanti, stop!" Bethanie says, a lot less subtle than her last warnings.

"It's a legit question. This restaurant is steep for a guy fresh out of school," Marco says, defending me. Or maybe he's preparing me for when the check comes and he won't be able to pay it.

"No trust fund or rich parents, but I have some money saved, at least until it runs out. Then I might have to pick up my old gambling habit again." Cole laughs, but no one else does. "How about your parents, Bethanie? What brought them to Colorado?"

Even though Cole is trying to evade me, I'd like to know the answer to that question myself.

"What makes you think they aren't from here?" Bethanie answers with another question, like she always does when anyone asks about her background.

"Oh, nothing. Just making conversation," Cole says. I can tell he's feeling the same deep freeze I get whenever I ask her about the Larsens.

"Have you become a Broncos fan yet?" Marco asks, changing the tone of the table, which, I'll admit, was getting a little tense.

"No way, man. Redskins till I die."

The entrée comes and I let Cole off the hook while he and Marco talk sports the way guys do when they have nothing in common but can become like brothers if they find a sport they both like. Listening to Cole talk, now I'm wondering if he's lying about his age. Like Bethanie accused me of acting, Cole talks and acts older than a guy fresh out of college—until he and Marco started talking sports. Now they sound like they can be the same age. Then again, that isn't much of a clue—my grandfather sounds the same way when he gets excited about the Atlanta Braves.

I wish I could ask Cole questions about that day in the bodega, but I haven't told Marco about that and don't plan to. Not only do he and his parents already think I'm just a walking trouble magnet, I'm also a little embarrassed that I didn't offer myself as a witness for the owner. It's something Marco would have done.

I don't have much to contribute conversationally until the lull between the main course and dessert, but then I get back to work.

"So, Cole, are you like Usher with just the one name?"

He laughs in a completely charming way that almost makes me want to back off. I can see why Bethanie is falling for him.

"Bethanie, I really like your friend—even if I feel a little like I'm meeting your parents."

"Oh no, this is way worse than meeting my parents. If you can survive Chanti, they won't be any problem at all."

"Good, because I want to meet them. I'll think of Chanti's interrogation as practice."

He wants to meet her parents? After knowing her less than a week? Freak. Freak with a disarming smile, but freak nonetheless.

"To answer your question, Chanti, I don't like last names. They denote ownership."

"Like slave names?" I ask. "I've heard my grandparents talk about that."

"Well, obviously not like a slave name. I mean the way it denotes your parents own you. Not even both your parents, but your father, really."

"That must be the weirdest thing I've ever heard," I say.

"It isn't weird to me, maybe because I went to second grade and learned how to interact with human beings," Bethanie says. "My father totally wants to own me."

"Really?" Cole says. He seems very interested in Bethanie's parents, her dad specifically. "You mean in that whole 'no one is good enough for my daughter' way?"

"No, I mean literally wants to own me. He . . ." Bethanie suddenly stops as though she realizes she was about to say too much.

"What were you going to say about your father?" Cole asks, taking a page from my book and trying to coax it out of her. I hope he has more luck because I've been dying to know what her family is hiding besides the lottery money.

Bethanie looks like she wants to talk—or confess—but doesn't know how to start. Cole and I both give her room and just stay quiet, but I guess Marco doesn't know the nuances of interrogation the way I, and apparently Cole, do.

"I'm lucky my pops and I get along well. Not all the time, but we're pretty good. I'm definitely proud to have his name. I know a lot of kids who see their parents as the bad guys but—"

"I'm surprised to hear that about Mr. Larsen," I say, interrupting Marco. I know it was rude, but I didn't want Bethanie to hold back just when it seemed she was about to talk. It might be my last chance to get some really good information tonight. "You and your dad seem so close."

"Wait, are you talking about some other man you *think* is my dad? Because we definitely aren't close. I wish we were like you and your father, Marco," Bethanie says. Then she fake-laughs and touches Cole's shoulder, obviously trying to reroute the conversation. "But he'll also play the 'no one is good enough for my daughter' routine. So you'd better be very charming when you meet him."

The moment is lost, but not because Cole and I didn't make an effort. I still don't trust him, but I'm beginning to think he might make a good sidekick in my effort to solve Bethanie's mystery.

"Oh, I don't think Cole will have any problem winning over your parents," I say, and turn to Marco just in time to notice a strange look on his face. The sexy smile that said *we share a secret* just a couple of minutes ago is gone. Long gone.

Maybe I *have* been too pushy with the questions. I can get a little focused when I'm on a case. Cole's interest in Bethanie's father makes me wonder if somehow he knows Mr. Larsen is Powerball rich and is using Bethanie to get to her dad's money. Now I just have to give Bethanie some real evidence because the girl is so sprung over this guy that she will never believe me. I stay quiet all through dessert, putting together clues that will give me the ammo to convince Bethanie I'm right.

Later, after Cole picks up the check and we're outside waiting for the valets to bring the cars, Marco pulls me aside. I'm sure Bethanie and Cole don't mind a bit, but I'm still keeping my eye on them.

"You were so quiet the last half of dinner, I thought maybe you were mad at me about something," Marco says.

"What? No way. I was just thinking about some of the things Cole said—you know, trying to figure out if his evasiveness was just mysterious charm or crazy stalker. I was just a little distracted."

"You mean like now?"

Oops. I guess he noticed I was still watching Bethanie and Cole when I should be concentrating on him. Marco is hot, it's a beautiful fall night, but I can't help myself when there's a mystery on my mind.

"Sorry, Marco. For the next three minutes until the valet brings your car, it's all about you and me."

"If you want, we could have more than three minutes. I was thinking maybe I could drive you home, then Bethanie doesn't have to go out of her way. I live pretty close to you; it would give us a chance to hang out, talk, and you know—whatever."

All of that was sounding really good until he said *and you know—whatever*, the part that worries me. No, I don't know *whatever* and I doubt I'll be any good at it—something I don't want Marco finding out, not after what Tasha told me.

"You know it's rude for a girl not to leave with the person she came with," I say, adding a light laugh and hoping I sound flirty instead of frigid.

"You know, I actually believed you set this up as a way for us to see each other, but now I'm beginning to think it really was all about that dude Cole."

"It was about checking out Cole *and* spending time with you. But letting Bethanie drive me home is a chance to learn more about what both of them are hiding. We girls love to rehash a double date."

"Right. Whatever. My car is here," Marco says when the valet pulls up in his old Grand Prix. He leaves me standing there without even saying good-bye.

Chapter 6

The next morning, my mind is still on the wrong boy. When I should be worrying about whether I was a little neglectful of Marco, I can't stop thinking about Cole. No, not *that* way. Everything about him has my BS detector going crazy. Yeah, he's cute and all man-of-the world (which isn't so hard to pull off when you're charming girls five years younger who are used to high school boys), but I can look past all of that to see that he's a liar. How perfect he and Bethanie will be together—two people who wouldn't tell the truth about themselves if someone paid them. Well, no one needs to pay me. I'm going to figure it out for free.

This morning, Lana caught me heading out of the house at the crack of way too early when she arrived home from a stakeout that went longer than planned. All she wanted was her bed and didn't question my story about going to Bethanie's house to work on a school project, or why I had to start so early. It's true that I'm going to Bethanie's house. I've been up since four o'clock thinking about Cole and the game he's running, so I figured I'd take the first bus over to her place to see what I can find out.

Just before I reach the bus stop on Center, I'm surprised

to run into MJ coming out of the bodega. I didn't even know it was open this early. She looks just as surprised to see me.

"What are you doing out this early on a Sunday?" she asks.

"Catching the bus to a friend's house. Gotta work on a school project."

"Y'all must be real dedicated to homework to start this early."

"It's a really complex project," I say, reading the sign on the door behind her. "The bodega doesn't open until seven. It's six thirty."

"And?"

"And I just saw you come out of there."

"I know the owner. Big Mama sent me for milk," she says, rubbing her hands together. It's a cold morning and she obviously didn't plan on being out very long since she's only wearing a fleece hoodie. No coat, gloves, or scarf—all required gear most Colorado mornings in mid-October.

"How do you know the owner?" I ask, not believing MJ even if I do trust her with my life.

"Dang, Chanti, always trying to get the 4-1-1. I *just* do, okay?" MJ says in a tone that says *back the hell off.*

But of course, I don't. "Where's the milk?"

"Look, Chanti, just 'cause I saved your butt and agreed to keep your mother's secret don't mean I'll let you question me like you some kind of five-o."

"I'm not trying to get in your business," I say, which is a complete lie, but I don't need MJ on my bad side and I'm actually hoping we can be friends again. "I'm just wondering about the owner because I was here when the bodega was held up last week."

"How you know about that?"

"I just said I was here when it happened. But you can't tell anyone. My mother would kill me if she found out."

MJ looks at me like she isn't sure she should believe me, and says, "Nobody knows about that holdup."

"Apparently you do. And as I said: *I. Was. Here.*"

I'm hoping that saying it slowly and with emphasis will make it sink in. I start walking toward the bus stop knowing MJ will follow since she doesn't think I should have information on the robbery. As much as I need to hear what she knows, I can't miss this bus. On Sundays, they don't run very often.

"MJ, you weren't involved, were you?"

"Hell no, I wasn't involved. I can't believe you would even ask me that. You know I'm straight now, getting my GED and all. I can't say how I know about it, I just do."

I figure it's no use pressing MJ for more, not now anyway. But if she knows something, I might be able to get it out of her by telling her what had me up so early thinking about Cole.

"Not that I'm an expert on robberies or anything, since this was the first one I've ever been in, but the whole thing felt off to me."

"Off like how?" MJ asks.

"How it happened in broad daylight, for one thing."

"Robberies happen during the day all the time," MJ says. "My ex tried to rob that bank in the middle of the day."

She's talking about the robbery that got her a two-year stint in juvie. I don't bring up the fact we've already determined her ex wasn't the brightest gangster out there, but stay focused on the bodega robbery.

"True, but everyone in Denver Heights knows that Friday afternoon is the absolute worst time to hold up the Center Street bodega because it's always packed with people buying tamales. But that day, the Friday Freebie line wasn't going out the door even with half an hour to go until they returned to full price."

"That don't mean anything. Maybe Tastee Treets was running a special and everyone was over there instead."

"Maybe. But then the regular cashier, the one who has *always* been there since I started high school or something, wasn't there."

"That's 'cause he's the owner's nephew," MJ says.

"Huh?"

"I mean that's why the same guy was always there. It's a family-owned business and the whole family works all the time."

"I guess maybe you do know the owner."

"I said I did," MJ says, sounding even more defensive than usual. Then she softens her tone and adds, "Big Mama knows the owner, okay? That's how come they let me in the store before opening."

That's plausible. Big Mama knows everyone. The owner is about the age of her average customer—MJ's grandmother runs an illegal betting game called the Numbers. She's sort of like the Godfather of Aurora Avenue, except she's gray-haired and she would never kill anyone. I don't think.

"Whether you know him or not, you have to admit it's coincidental that he picks the very day of the robbery to take time off. So did the lady who usually helps out on Fridays. And who is this new cashier, anyway? When did they hire him—just in time for the nephew to take the day off? Then they make him start work—alone—on the busiest day of the week. It's also curious that I haven't seen him in there since."

"First you ask if I'm involved. Now you think Eddie had something to do with it?"

"Who is Eddie?" MJ has me totally confused.

"Look," MJ says, pointing behind me. "I see your bus coming."

I turn around and see the bus, but it's still two blocks away, and I really want to know whether Eddie is the owner's nephew, the new cashier, or someone entirely new in this convoluted story MJ's telling. And why the nephew wasn't there that day and why the new guy was gone when the cops arrived after Ada called them. Most importantly, I want to know what MJ knows and why she's holding out on me, but by the time I turn around to ask her, she's twenty yards down the block, yelling, "Catch you later, Chanti."

As if this robbery wasn't strange enough already, now I can add MJ somehow being connected to the list of oddities. Cole showing up in the middle of it looking like he got lost on his way to a polo match might actually be the least bizarre part of the weirdness. That's what I'm thinking when I ring Bethanie's doorbell. Her mother answers after a few minutes, and it's obvious I woke her. Her hair's smashed in on one side and she hasn't done her makeup yet. I have never seen Mrs. Larsen without full makeup. No matter the occasion or time of day, she looks like the victim of an overzealous cosmetics counter lady who is a frustrated makeup artist for a reason. I also have never seen Mrs. Larsen without at least one item of animal print clothing on, and this record still stands.

She is holding together her leopard print robe to keep from revealing the zebra print pajamas underneath. Animal print is great, but even fashion-challenged me knows head-to-toe is a definite don't. When I first met Bethanie, I couldn't figure out why she had so much money and wanted so desperately to fit in with the Langdon rich, but could never quite pull off that effortless style and snobbishness that the born rich must have stamped on their DNA. Until I met her parents, saw her house, and learned about their lottery fortune. Then it all made perfect sense.

"Honey, do you realize how early it is? Something better be on fire for you to get me out the bed this early on a Sunday morning."

"Sorry, Mrs. Larsen. I thought it would be okay. Most people are up by now."

"Most people have jobs or religion. I ain't got either one. Bethanie is asleep, but you're welcome to go up and ruin her morning, too."

Then she left me standing in the door and went back upstairs, all that animal-printed polyester flowing behind her. If they ever made a *Real Housewives of Denver*, Mrs. Larsen would totally get the part of rich-but-tacky-diva-you-best-not-piss-off.

"Wake up, Bethanie."

My command is met with silence. I try again and see some progress because this time she grunts.

"Look, I brought your favorite chai from the coffeehouse. I had to get off the bus two stops early for that, Bethanie."

"What the hell are you doing here? And why are you calling me that?"

"Because it's your name," I say, though I've always figured it was an alias. I'm hoping in her semiconscious state she'll prove me right, but I'm not that lucky.

"What are you doing here so early?" she asks, sitting up.

"I thought you might want to talk some more about dinner last night."

That gets her attention and she pops up as though she'd never been asleep. She looks a hotter mess than her mom did. Of course, no one looks good fresh out of a deep sleep, but I've never seen her looking anything but magazine-cover ready. Even if her style is a little much, Bethanie is really pretty. She's got that whole exotic-girl look the magazines like. You know, when they want a black girl for diversity but they don't want her to be *too* much of a black girl—full lips but not *too* full, wide nose but not *too* wide, brown skin but not *too* brown. I'll never be on anyone's cover because I'm *too* all of that, plus some. That's fine by me because I think I'm kinda cute, which is probably far less expensive and worrisome than being beautiful.

But now Bethanie looks like a mere mortal, like the rest

of us. I must not hide my shock, because she tells me not to go anywhere and heads for the attached bathroom. I thought she'd just brush her teeth and splash some water on her face, but when I hear the shower go on, I'm glad for the opportunity to snoop.

I have limits—no drawer opening, no diary reading, but anything in plain sight is fair game, which is how I learned her dad is not really a rich oilman like the Larsens play off to the rest of the world. I saw a letter from the lottery commission on their kitchen counter and called Bethanie on it. It was weird. She got mad when she realized I knew the truth about her family (or some of it), but then we actually became better friends. She didn't have to play the rich socialite around me anymore, and I learned we're more alike than not. She won't tell me anything about herself that happened before her dad picked six winning numbers, but I do know she'd fit in better on Aurora Avenue than she does in this swanky Cherry Creek neighborhood.

There isn't really much to go on. The room doesn't have that lived in, been here forever feel to it, which makes sense because I don't think Bethanie has lived here very long despite her efforts to make me think otherwise. Every now and then her accent goes all country grammar. The only personalized space in the room is a big corkboard hanging on the wall over her desk. There are photos of Bethanie and her parents, with her ranging in age from maybe six or seven to now. They must be vacation pictures because they're all shot outside and in various locales: palm trees and ocean; mountains and snow; cactus and desert. These are the only photos—no pictures of other family members or of Bethanie's friends.

For Bethanie to be so romance-crazy that she keeps reading *Romeo and Juliet* over and over, I'm surprised there isn't a single photo of a boyfriend or crush. I don't have much experience in that department, but I imagined Bethanie was something like Michelle, who is such a romantic she thinks all those men going in and out of Ada Crawford's house are boyfriends. Michelle has all kinds of boy-related stuff in her room: movie stubs from dates, photos of boys she dated or crushed on, even a couple of love notes written on actual paper. Last month, just so she could meet some Langdon guys, Bethanie tricked me into going to the party where I was set up for that crime I didn't commit. So what if she didn't know I was going to be set up. She still conned me in the name of romance, making the lack of boyfriend evidence in her room a little strange.

Also on the board are school mementos, things like sports team banners, school decals, announcements for dances and fund-raisers, spirit buttons—the usual school stuff. What's unusual is that the keepsakes are from so many different schools. It seems like a weird thing to collect—mementos from schools you didn't attend. Bethanie must be really good at something because there are lots of blue ribbons pinned to the board. I have ribbons like this from science fair every year since sixth grade, but nowhere near this many. I unpin a batch of ribbons from the board and look at the back of one, only to find the little card usually attached to this kind of ribbon—the card that says what the contest was, the date it took place, where it was held—has been torn off. I look through all the ribbons and find the card has been torn off all of them.

I didn't get the ribbons back up on the board a second too soon because Bethanie comes out of the bathroom, looking like the girl I know, jumps on her bed, and starts sipping the chai, probably cool by now. If this was Tasha's room, I'd join her on the bed, but Bethanie and I aren't that tight, so I pull the chair from her desk a little closer and take a seat.

"Isn't Cole everything I told you he was? A real gentleman despite how rude you were to him."

"I thought I was there to check him out, and that's what I did."

"So?"

"So . . . I think you're falling too fast. You don't know enough about him."

"And you do after spending a single dinner with him?"

"That's all *you've* spent with him. I was there when you met him, remember? And don't tell me about all your hours on the phone. It's almost like texting. Someone can be a whole different person when you aren't face-to-face. For that matter, people can hide a lot even when you are."

"You mean me."

"I mean Cole." Well yeah, I meant her.

Bethanie is quiet for a second, sipping her chai to stall while she thinks of how to say whatever she's about to say. I don't try to fill the silence. Lana says you learn the most from a perp not from questioning him but from letting him just speak his mind. Bethanie isn't a perp, but I have to treat her like one if I want to get some information out of her.

"Before Marco, I'm guessing you didn't really have a lot of boyfriends."

Bethanie is being generous in calling Marco my boyfriend, and we both know it. She is definitely trying to tread lightly.

"I haven't had a boyfriend because I'm not into serious," I say. "I figured there are too many fine men out there to waste my time on one."

"Men?"

"You know what I mean." How could she? I don't even know what I mean; I'm just trying to sound like I know what the hell I'm talking about.

"So you must know a lot about boys."

At first I think she's being sarcastic seeing how she's always trying to give me advice on Marco, but I realize she's serious. Did she actually believe my story about never having one boyfriend because I'd rather play around? She might be a blue ribbon winner of something, but she'd never be a great detective. Or even a mediocre one.

"I know enough," I say, going along with it.

"I wish I did. I've never even been on a date until last night."

Okay, I was blowing up my knowledge about boys a little, but at least I've been on a few dates, even if they were lame setups by Tasha that didn't lead to second dates. Once I get past how honest a girl has to be to admit that to someone after pretending she's a pro on the subject, I wonder how Bethanie could be about to turn seventeen and never have had a date. Between her looks, the car, and her money, surely she could have attracted some guy, even if for the wrong reasons. I try to act like I'm not as surprised as I am, but she reads my mind.

"It's because of my dad. He's always been super-protective of me, especially when it comes to boys."

"All fathers are like that," I say, not that I would know since I never met my father. Lana was almost sixteen when she got pregnant; he was seventeen and didn't want anything to do with Lana or being a dad. Because they only got together one time, he even suggested he might not be the father. *My* father. Conveniently for him, just a few days after Lana confirmed she was pregnant, his military parents—who she suspects were never told about me—had their posts reassigned. Lana says it was convenient for her, too, because he was no one she wanted to raise a kid with. We never talk about him; it's like he never existed. That means I only have Tasha and Michelle's fathers to go on, and in Michelle's case, her father's a preacher and crazy strict. That still didn't keep her having her first time with Donnell Down the Street, Aurora Ave.'s resident thug. So even without firsthand experience, I know fathers get crazy about their daughters, and somehow the daughters still manage to hook up if they really want to.

"I'm pretty sure nobody's father is like mine when it

comes to protecting me. And now with the money, he's just over-the-top crazy about it."

"I'm guessing he doesn't know about last night, then."

"He thinks I was hanging out with you, which is true."

"So you only asked me to double date so I could be your alibi?"

"It's not like I committed a crime," Bethanie says. "Even if my dad might think I did."

"He has to know you want to date. I mean, you're almost an adult."

"Yeah, almost an adult and afraid to go on my first date without you and Marco there," she says, looking like I'd feel after sharing something like that—completely exposed. It's something you could only tell a real friend.

"If it helps, you were a lot better at dating than I am, and I have some experience."

It was true. She knew just what to say, managed to make her guy feel smart and interesting while being smart and interesting herself. Instead of focusing on the lies Cole was telling, I should have been taking notes.

"Thanks—it does help. I really like Cole."

I stand up and walk over to the corkboard with its oddly unexpected mementos and missing the ones you'd expect to see, and pretend to look at it as though I'm seeing it for the first time.

"You don't really want me to tell you what I think about Cole, do you?" I ask. "You never did."

"No. Especially now because I have a feeling I'm not going to like it."

Chapter 7

I did keep my opinion to myself, though I'm even more worried about Bethanie than ever. No wonder she's falling for the guy. Cole would be hard not to fall for even if he weren't good-looking and completely charming. Work that magic on a girl who has never been on a date, and it's all over for her. Not unless I can come up with a way to make her see that's all the more reason to slow down. Which is also what I wish Lana would do at this very minute. She's giving me a ride to school and while I appreciate not having to take the bus, I'd also like to hold on to my breakfast. Lana drives like she's still a uniform cop on her way to a bank robbery. It's especially bad this morning since she's running late for an early meeting with her boss. I figure a conversation might remind her that her only child is in the car, and she'll take it a little slower.

"Lana, have you ever had to tell a friend bad news about a guy?"

"Every woman has to at some point, if she's any kind of real friend."

"So you're saying I should do it?"

"If you care about her. I told my best friend in high school that her boyfriend had come on to me. I gave her the exact words he used. I can't remember them now, but he made it clear what he was about."

"And she broke up with him?" I ask, noticing Lana does seem to be taking it easier on the turns.

"No, she broke up with me. Being honest doesn't mean she'll take the news the way you hope."

"She believed him over you, even though y'all were girls?"

"One day you'll fall in love and learn just how stupid it can make you, at least at first. Sometimes the love is worth being momentarily stupid; sometimes you figure out it wasn't at all."

"When I told Michelle her boyfriend was a loser, she didn't take it very well."

"But you turned out to be right."

"Yeah, but everyone on the street knew Donnell was a loser, everyone except Michelle. I didn't feel bad at all about busting him."

"You don't have any evidence to show your friend about whoever the latest loser is?"

"All circumstantial. Barely even that—more like a hunch."

"You might want more than a hunch before you go messing with love."

"I suppose. But what if my hunch tells me it's urgent and that I don't have time to get better proof?"

"Believe it or not, I remember what it's like to be your age. Everything was urgent, and now I can't even remember what half the fuss was about. Unless she's in some kind of danger, you can wait."

Well, I don't think Bethanie is in danger of anything but a shrinking bank account, so I suppose I should take Lana's advice.

"It sucks that your friend dumped you because you told the truth."

"It broke my heart. But, fortunately, she figured out that

the guy wasn't worth it. A few years later, I was a bridesmaid in her wedding to a guy who was."

I'm so glad Lana's story has a happy ending, and I tell her so before I get out of the car. Bethanie and I aren't BFFs yet, but she's the closest friend I have at Langdon, and in a place where I couldn't fit in even if I felt like trying, an ally is a necessity. Since I started Langdon, I've been pretty much a pariah with everyone—the headmistress, teachers, the popular kids—especially the popular kids. I would have transferred to North High the minute Lana gave me the chance if it wasn't for Bethanie and Marco.

Between every class, I hang out at Bethanie's locker because I've decided she can handle hearing what I have to say. She's only known Cole a week, definitely not enough time to be in love with him, let alone reach the point of stupid over him. But now it's fifth period and I still haven't seen her. I try her cell, and she doesn't answer.

"Miss Evans."

Oh no. I've caught the attention of Headmistress Smythe, which is a lot like catching a bad case of the flu—it takes forever to shake and makes you miserable until you do.

"I've seen you here at Miss Larsen's locker every period since first bell. I take it that means you know nothing of her whereabouts."

"What do you mean?"

"I mean she didn't come to school today and her parents didn't call to excuse her. Repeated calls to her home have gone unanswered."

"I haven't seen her all day, either."

"Bethanie seems like a well-adjusted girl. I know that even the best students can be led astray by certain influences."

I don't have to ask her if the certain influence she's referring to is me.

"If I hear from Bethanie, I'll ask her to check in at the front office. Now I'd better get to Western Civ."

On my way to class, I send Bethanie a text asking her what's up. She responds that I should meet her outside the coffeehouse after school—she has something to tell me.

Bethanie pulls up in front of the coffeehouse and tells me to get in. "I don't want to risk anyone from school seeing me," she says, like she's on some undercover mission.

"You mean because you skipped?"

"You noticed?"

"So did Smythe. If you're going to skip, at least know how to do it. Either fake sick to your mom so she can let them know you'll be out, or you should've called the office pretending to be your mom. I'm pretty sure Smythe called your house."

"So what if she did?"

"You've made it your mission to get on Smythe's good side, especially now that her Queen Suck-Up has been kicked out of school. I thought your plan was to take over that spot in the Langdon hierarchy."

"I don't care about Smythe or Langdon Prep anymore," Bethanie says, parking the car on a quiet side street a few blocks from the coffeehouse.

"So what happened between Friday and today, because that was your big plan three days ago."

"Love is what happened," she says.

I guess I was wrong about her not having time to get stupid over that guy. I stay quiet for a second, thinking how to handle this. What I want to say is *Have you completely lost your mind?* But that never works when Lana says it to me, and only pisses me off.

"Wow, that was kind of quick."

"We spent the day together."

"Doing . . ."

"Not what you think. Cole is a complete gentleman," she

says, reaching behind my seat to pull out a bag from the floor. "He bought me these chocolates. Want one?"

"I always want chocolate," I say, taking a truffle from the box even if it is from a stalker. Yum, a stalker with great taste in expensive chocolate.

"It wasn't even planned. I was parking my car this morning in my usual spot and he showed up."

Bethanie has yet to come clean about the lie she used to get into Langdon—that she's broke and needed one of the three scholarships they gave to three broke kids at the beginning of the school year. Marco and I were the other two, and we actually are broke. Bethanie wanted in to Langdon so badly she was willing to lie her way in since they normally don't admit students after ninth grade. She claims she's telling Smythe the truth soon and repaying the scholarship money, but first she wants to make sure she's in Smythe's good graces. Lying on the scholarship application is probably a serious violation of the Langdon Prep honor code. It would kind of suck if she's made all this effort and ends up expelled. I keep telling her she has the kind of money that makes people overlook honor codes and admission rules, but Bethanie says one scam is enough. Until she becomes Smythe's favorite student without using bribes, Bethanie parks a quarter mile from school so no one sees that brand-new BMW she's driving.

"How does he know where you park?"

"I don't know," Bethanie says, then goes quiet for a second, probably thinking it was a little strange that he knew where she parked. But she doesn't think about it long enough for it to register that the guy must be casing her. "However he knew, it was a good thing."

"Why?"

"There was some guy already parked in my spot, leaning against his car. Even though he was pushing a brand-new Jag, he looked like someone straight off my old block back home—nobody I wanted to mess with, right?"

"Where exactly would that be?"

She ignores my question.

"For a second, I actually thought I knew him—he was kind of familiar. I parked behind him and got out of my car. Dude just stares at me, like he was waiting for me. Then he actually says, 'I've been waiting for you' and starts coming toward me."

"What? You've got two guys stalking you now?"

She ignores that comment, too.

"Cole pulled up at just that moment."

"See what I mean? He *is* stalking you."

"He was just coming to Langdon to try to catch me on my way into school."

"But the street you park on is not on the way to Langdon. You'd have to live around here just to know it even exists."

"Would you just let me finish my story?"

"All right," I say, helping myself to another piece of chocolate.

"So Cole rolls down his window and tells me to get in. Then he gives that guy a look that sends him running back to his car."

"Cole doesn't strike me as being so tough he could send a guy like you described running to his car."

"Okay, maybe not *running,* but he did back off. Then Cole talked me into hanging out with him. He didn't like the looks of that guy and thought maybe he should watch out for me the rest of the day. First we had breakfast at that little café on First Street—"

"Hello? Do you think your itinerary is what we should be discussing here?"

"What—you mean that guy?"

"Yeah, that guy. Who is he, and why would he be waiting for you? And going back to the very beginning, what about Cole knowing where you went to school?"

"You were there when he explained that, Chanti."

"Even if I bought that story, which I don't, what about today and him being in the right place at the right time at your out-of-the-way parking spot? For the second time in less than two weeks, I might add."

Bethanie looks at me like she's confused.

"Come on, Bethanie—the bodega robbery? Not to be profiling, but what's a guy like Cole doing at that bodega?"

"You mean a gallant guy? A brave guy?"

"I mean a *white* guy. Not like an Eminem-wannabe-looking-for-street-cred white guy, either. One who looks like he came out of a Tommy Hilfiger ad, or your side of town."

"Well, I was at the bodega and I *am* from my side of town."

"We both know that's only because your dad picked the right six numbers. If you were being straight with me, you'd admit you're more comfortable in the Heights than in Cherry Creek. Plus, you were giving me a ride home that day. You had a reason to be over there."

"Cole could've had a reason to be there, too. Maybe he was passing through and needed something to eat."

"People like Cole don't pass through the Heights, they avoid it. That bodega—my whole neighborhood—might as well have a sign at the entrance that says RICH-LOOKING WHITE GUYS ENTER AT YOUR OWN RISK. But he was up in there like he owned the place. I don't know, maybe he really is that fierce, but he doesn't strike me as stupid."

"So what are you saying?"

"I'm saying that it was weird how the BOGO tamale line just seemed to disappear after he came in, even though it's usually out the door until five o'clock."

"You think he somehow made all the people disappear so he wouldn't have to wait in line for a free tamale? I'm pretty sure he can afford to buy one. And those tamales aren't *that* great."

She's wrong about those tamales, which are like heaven wrapped in pork and masa. But I want to stay on track because I'm about to say what I really think and I'm hoping she won't blow me off the way Lana's friend did.

"No, I'm saying maybe he staged that robbery and was working with the junkie. The *alleged* junkie. Not only that, I'd never seen that cashier before and haven't seen him since," I say, though I'm thinking that guy won't be such a mystery once I get MJ to talk. "Maybe he had someone outside the store sending the crowd away or—"

"And got the store owners to go along with the whole thing?"

"I haven't figured that part out, but he must have somehow."

"Paranoid much, Chanti? Why would he ever do that?"

"For the same reason he planted that scary dude in your parking spot and then showed up just in time to save the day."

"Forget paranoid. Now you're just crazy."

"He's trying to get close to you, to gain your trust."

"Most guys just ask for your number or find you online."

"Not if they need to gain your trust quickly."

"And why would he need to do that? I know I'm inexperienced with the whole dating game, but I do know guys usually don't stage dangerous situations just so they can rescue the girl they want," she says, then pauses for a second. "Although that would be crazy romantic, right?"

"No, I don't think that's it."

"You think he's so mad about me he can't wait to do the usual dating routine, or he wants me so bad he's trying to skip past all the bases and move straight to home?"

Okay, here goes the part where she's probably never going to speak to me again.

"I think it's because he wants your money."

Bethanie looks as hurt as I expected her to be. I would,

too, if my friend just told me the guy I'm getting stupid over doesn't want me, that he only wants my money.

"You said yourself he's rich-looking. You've seen his car."

"No I haven't."

"Oh, that's right. The restaurant valet brought my car first. Believe me, it's not something a broke dude would drive."

"Well, even if he has some money, how did he get it? He told us his family doesn't have money and he isn't independently wealthy, even if that's the story you made up for him before you actually met him. Maybe this is how he does it, scamming rich girls."

"You're crazy."

"But it's a lot of money, Bethanie."

"You're crazy and jealous. And a bi-atch."

Then she tells me to get the hell out of her car. Yeah, that didn't go well at all.

Chapter 8

I'm definitely not crazy. If Cole isn't after Bethanie's money, he's after something, and it isn't only her heart. And I'm pretty sure I'm not a bi-atch, even though I probably could have presented my theory better. I should have framed it in some positive language like my teacher tells us to do before we rip apart someone's masterpiece in Creative Writing class. Jealous? That one I might be slightly guilty of. Not jealous of what Bethanie and Cole have because, really, it's only been two weeks. More like jealous of Bethanie's confidence. She's probably the only girl on the planet with less boy experience, but she's fearless compared to me. She knows what she wants and she's fighting to get it, even if her only friend is giving her a thousand reasons not to. I have what I wanted but I'm afraid to enjoy it, and now I'm pretty sure Marco's angry with me.

That's when I get the idea of getting off my bus a few stops early to go by Marco's house to find out just how angry. Bethanie's drama gives me a reason to see him, tell him my concern for her, before his parents get home from work. I've never been inside his house since his parents ended our romance before it could truly get started, but I know where he lives.

When Marco opens the door and finds me there, he

doesn't seem super excited. But he does look super cute, and that gives me the strength to go on.

"Can we talk for a minute?"

"I don't think it's a good idea. My parents will be home soon."

"I'll be gone before they get home. I just need to talk to someone."

"Is something wrong? Are you okay?" he asks in a way that just about makes me butter.

"I'm fine, but I'm really worried about Bethanie."

"Hold on a sec."

He reaches somewhere just inside the door and finds a coat, then comes out onto his porch instead of letting me in. It's one of those October days in Colorado that start at sixty-five degrees and drop to forty by the time school ends. They fool me every time. Going inside would have been better, but I'll take what I can get.

"What's wrong with Bethanie?"

"There's a lot wrong and I'm not sure how to fix it."

"Let's sit on the swing," he says, putting his coat around my shoulders. It smells like him, and I just want to sit there a minute and breathe him in. It's as close as we've gotten since the Kiss. "Tell me what's up."

"It's Cole."

He slides away from me and I swear the look on his face suggests he might even want his coat back.

"You came over here to talk about some other dude? Isn't he Bethanie's boyfriend?"

"Yeah, of course. You were there at the restaurant."

"Oh, did you notice?"

So I guess I'm not the only one who realized I was a little negligent at dinner.

"I wasn't the best date, was I?"

"If you can call it a date. Toward the end, you barely said three words to me. But you had plenty to say to him."

"Of course I did. That's why I was asking Cole all those questions. I wanted to figure out his game."

"Whenever Bethanie and I tried to say anything, you somehow moved the conversation back to him. When you weren't asking him questions, you were hanging on his every word."

"I was trying to place his accent. Did you notice how it kept changing? He claims he hasn't lived in Atlanta for a long time but—"

"Chanti, you're doing it again."

"Doing what?"

"Did you come to see me or to talk about some other guy?"

"Both. I went out with them to see if he was some kind of con man and now I'm pretty sure he is."

"When you asked me to do the double date thing, I thought it was just an excuse to ask me out, one that my parents might buy into if they found out I was with you. But you made it clear at dinner that it really was about you checking out Cole."

"I told you it was about both things. I just did a better job at one than the other. But I promise I'll make it up."

"Your interest in that dude went way beyond looking out for a friend."

Uh, what? Where did that come from, and is that what he's been thinking since Saturday?

"You think I have an interest in Cole beyond figuring out if he was conning Bethanie?"

"Like you said—I was there. Bethanie and I could have set our napkins on fire and neither of you would have noticed."

"What?"

"Don't tell me you didn't see that. Whatever game you were playing, he was playing right along with you."

"No, I didn't see that, but if you did, it only confirms

what a con he is. Cons love the game, the whole cat-and-mouse thing of being suspected but not getting caught."

Marco looks at me like I'm crazy. "I know you solved those crimes at school and kept us out of jail, but you do realize you're not actually a cop, right?"

"Right," I say weakly, realizing I *do* sound a little crazy to someone who doesn't know why I'm the way I am—having a secret undercover cop for a mom.

"Seemed to me the double date was set up with the wrong partners."

"The guy said I was observant and had a keen ear—not exactly love talk. Marco, I promise no one was into anyone at that table."

"I was into you, and Bethanie was into him. But you and Cole weren't playing along."

Okay, this is just crazy talk. Or just a guy who can't tell flirting from spying. If Bethanie agreed with Marco's take on that night, surely she wouldn't have told me what she did about Cole. Or maybe that's why she did. Maybe she thinks I was scamming on Cole and she wanted to make sure I knew he was hers. After all, she did call me a bi-atch.

"I swear you have this completely wrong. It was just a little detective work I was doing."

"All right. Let's say that was it—"

"Because it really *was*."

"Then I still wasn't the one you wanted to be with that night, was I?"

It didn't sound right the way he said it, though I had to agree. Except I don't—I just stay quiet.

"I don't get it, Chanti. You know my parents think you're trouble after what happened with Donnell. I keep telling them how great you are and how that was just one case of wrong place, wrong time. But you keep trying to find trouble. You're making it hard for my parents to come around to you."

"I'm really glad you're defending me to them, but I also have to defend Bethanie."

"Did she ask you to? And defend her from what—a guy with a weird accent?"

"No, she didn't. But it's more than just the accent."

"Just tell me one real thing this guy has done to make you willing to give up whatever we have going?"

Whatever we have going? Don't we *know* what we have going?

"I was right about the burglary ring, wasn't I?"

"That was different. It was before us."

"It was how we got to be us."

He looks at me like he wants to say something else, but doesn't. I can think of a thousand ways to fill up the space of the words he doesn't say, and none of them good.

"I'd better get going, I guess. Your parents will be coming."

"Yeah, good idea," he says as he takes his coat from my shoulders. "See you around school."

Is it my imagination, or did that sound like a breakup?

Chapter 9

Marco and Bethanie both stayed clear of me at school for the rest of the week. Marco knows my schedule and somehow managed to avoid the hallways where he knew I'd be, and went to lunch with his football friends. Bethanie's avoidance was less calculated. She just hasn't been to school most of the week. I learned from Mildred, our head custodian and my favorite Langdon informant, that Bethanie showed up in the nurse's office a couple of times claiming illness and then went home. Except I'm pretty sure she didn't go home. I'm not the only one who suspects she's ditching to hang out with Cole, because when I check my messages between classes, there's one from Mrs. Larsen, asking if I might talk to her after school. It must be serious because she even offers to pick me up from Langdon, saying she'll be here at four either way and that she hopes I'll be waiting.

I'm used to taking the bus and making the long walk to the stop, so it seems weird waiting in the circle in front of school for someone to pick me up, especially when it's Bethanie's mom. It's four on the dot when a Bentley pulls into the circle. I have never seen a Bentley in real life, not even at Langdon, but I know the grille anywhere because it's in just about every rap video ever made in this century. I'm

interested in who might be inside it, but not as interested as I
am in where Mrs. Larsen is. She's already made me wait half
an hour after last bell. Then the Bentley driver's door opens
and a man gets out. Given the nondescript black suit and tie,
and plain white shirt, he's either coming from his job as
G-man or he's a driver. Now I really want to know which
Langdonite this car belongs to, and I watch to see which of
the few remaining kids hanging around will go to the Bentley, but no one does. Color me shocked when the driver
walks up the stairs to where I'm sitting and says my full name.

"Uh, yes?"

"Mrs. Larsen is waiting in the car."

You're probably imagining he's talking to me with a
British accent, right? Because I always imagined if I had a car
like that, and a driver to go with it, he'd be British with a
name like Jeeves or Giles. But not this dude. He is straight off
the block: six feet four, two hundred and seventy-five pounds
of muscle, shaved head, bling in both ears. When he says my
name, it sounds more Lil Jon than Jeeves, especially the way
he put *Yo* in front of it. I'm thinking I'm not going anywhere
with this guy, until I see Mrs. Larsen in the backseat of the
Bentley after she rolls down her tinted window. Every time I
see this woman, I understand a little better where Bethanie
gets her drama. The driver grabs my backpack and heads for
the car. I follow, not that I have a choice if I want my stuff
back.

"I'm glad you waited for me," Mrs. Larsen says, all Southern magnolia as usual. "I'm sorry to make you wait half an
hour, but I didn't want to risk Bethanie seeing us."

"But Bethanie wasn't . . ."

"Yes?"

"Right. That was a good idea."

Even though Bethanie won't talk to me, I figured I
wouldn't bust her just yet. Besides, staying silent is always the
best way to get people to spill their secrets—people can't stand

silence. And I get the feeling the Larsens have plenty of secrets.

We get to their house in under five minutes. I never realized how close to Langdon Bethanie lived, even though I've been to the house a couple of times. I guess it's because I've never gone there straight from school and I still don't know the area all that well. When you take the bus, that's pretty much the only route you know.

"You live really close by. Why does Bethanie drive to school?"

"Oh, she loves that car. I guess she wants to show it off."

Yeah, except no one but Marco and I knows she drives it. Apparently she still hasn't told her parents how she got into Langdon, either. They still think it's because she's rich, when it's the complete opposite.

"If you were afraid of her catching us at school, aren't you also afraid she'll see us here together?" I ask Mrs. Larsen after she's invited me to have a seat in the "salon" (the living room for the rest of us) and told the maid, Molly, to bring me a Coke. The maid is different than the woman I met the last time I was here. The new chick looks like the female version of the driver, as big as MJ and just as tough-looking. The Larsens must hire their domestic staff from the Thugs-R-Us employment agency.

"She didn't tell you about her after-school charity work?"

"No, she didn't."

"She just started that a couple of days ago. She goes straight there from school and works two hours. I'm surprised she didn't tell you."

"So am I."

The maid comes in with my Coke, followed by Mr. Larsen. Whenever I see Bethanie's parents together, I always think of Betty and Barney Rubble because he's a good four inches shorter than Mrs. Larsen, who isn't super tall or anything.

"I'm glad you came to talk to us about Bethanie's situation," Mr. Larsen says, taking a seat on the sofa next to his wife.

"Her situation?"

"I hadn't said anything to her about that yet," Mrs. Larsen says, seeming miffed that her husband was stepping on her lines. "Honestly, I'm glad she started this charity work thing because between that and school, maybe she won't have time to spend with that boy she's been seeing."

"So you know about Cole?"

"Is that his name?" Mr. Larsen says. "See, already you know more than we do. What can you tell us about him?"

Just then the driver comes into the room and leans against the fireplace, which looks like it has never once held a fire. There's a gold-gilded cherub where a pile of wood should be, and he's spouting a plastic floral arrangement from his mouth. The first time I came to Bethanie's house, before I even knew about her Powerball ticket, I knew from her family's decor that they were ghetto-rich and not at all used to money. A month later, that still hasn't changed.

"Now just wait, Lola Mae," says Mr. Larsen. "We don't want the girl to think she's being interrogated."

Lola Mae? I knew they were from the South, but I didn't think they were also from the 1920s.

"Nobody's interrogating her," Mrs. Larsen protests. "I just have some questions to ask, is all."

"That *is* a little how it feels," I say, looking at the driver, who is definitely adding to that feeling. Working a toothpick between his teeth, he crosses his tree-trunk arms and stares at me like he wants to do me bodily harm. Definitely not a Jeeves.

"We're just concerned whenever E . . ."

"Who?"

"Bethanie, I mean. That's what we call her for short."

"Just *E*?" I ask, because I don't know how they get *E* out of *Bethanie*. Seems like it would be *B* if anything, like Beyoncé's nickname. But Mr. Larsen keeps talking as though he didn't hear me ask for clarification.

"We're just concerned whenever she has a new friend."

"People make new friends all the time," I say.

"Yes, well, Bethanie is special, you see."

I do see. So is this entire family, and not in a good way.

"If she's in school and is now going to do this charity work, when does she have time to even be with him?" I ask.

"It isn't that she spends so much time with him," says Mrs. Larsen. "It's the hold he seems to have over her in such a short time. She never mentions his name, but he's all she talks about. Like she wants to keep his name a secret."

"You mean when she's even talking to us," says Mr. Larsen. "Soon as she comes home, she goes straight to her room, won't talk to us at all. She didn't used to be like that. We figured the change was due to this boy."

"Mr. Larsen, you keep a pretty tight leash on Bethanie, right?"

"Is that what she told you?"

"Something like that."

"It's for her own good. When she asked for that car, instead of having Tiny drive her to school, I let her, didn't I, Mama?"

Molly and Tiny. Seriously, these names have to be just as made up as *Bethanie*.

"I think that may be the problem," Mr. Larsen continues. "We give her too much. She thinks having money makes her grown. I should cut back her allowance. What do regular kids make for allowance these days, Chanti?"

"I don't really get allowance. I had a job until recently, and I'll probably start looking for another one soon."

"Oh, that's right. You're poor," Mrs. Larsen says, shaking her head like she just learned I've come down with an incurable disease. I want to remind them that until recently, they were broke, too. But I stay quiet because Bethanie doesn't want them to know I know about the lottery ticket.

"Well, I think maybe we overindulged her," Mr. Larsen says. "Whatever the going rate is, I'm pretty sure it isn't a thousand a week."

I try not to spray a mouthful of Coke all over them.

"Yeah, it's safe to assume that is nowhere near the going rate for 'regular' kids," I say after I recover from that information. "Maybe she's just breaking out a little. It's like when I go on the cabbage soup diet. Once I get my first taste of chocolate after a week of cabbage soup, I can't just stop at one piece."

The Larsens stare at me like I'm speaking Farsi. Since my analogy is clearly lost on them, I try a different approach. The truth.

"Let's just be frank," I say, because I have always wanted to say that and this seems as good a time as any. "You're worried this guy is after your money, right?"

"My money? My money," Mr. Larsen says twice, like this thought never occurred to him. Then he smiles at his wife and slaps his leg. "Yes, the money."

I take a big swig of Coke and actually hope Bethanie walks in right this moment so she can translate her family's madness for me. And to reassure me Tiny is not an escaped serial killer.

"Did you have other concerns about Cole besides him being a potential gold digger? You know, since you're in oil and everything."

"No, young lady, we shared the same exact concern as you. A father can't be too careful about his pride and joy."

I wouldn't know, but nod in agreement.

"Still, we would be very appreciative if you could talk to her, maybe warn her against getting too caught up with this boy. She might listen to you."

Mr. Larsen seems so relieved that all Cole is after is his

money, I don't have the heart to tell him his daughter probably wants nothing to do with me, or that it's too late—she's
already too caught up with Cole. When he asks Tiny to drive
me home, I decline because I'm not sure I want to be in a car
alone with Tiny. But no use hurting anybody's feelings, so I
tell them a Bentley rolling through Denver Heights would
surely get us jacked, which amuses Tiny enough that he actually cracks a smile. After many protests between Mrs. Larsen
and me about how I'm getting home, I agree to let Mr. Larsen
drop me at the nearest bus stop. Once I'm finally on the
crosstown bus, I make mental notes of all the things about
this visit that will become part of my file on this case, because
it has definitely become a case.

Chapter 10

Lana is on the sofa watching a *Perry Mason* marathon one of the cable channels runs every Saturday. She loves watching crime shows even though she gets to live it in real life every day, but without the slam-dunk ease the cops solve cases with on TV. I take a seat beside her, trying to figure out how to ask her questions I have about my case without letting her know I'm working one. Lana's proud of me for keeping myself out of jail by solving the case I was arrested for, but she's in agreement with Marco's parents that I tend to attract trouble.

She'd prefer I'd not go looking for any. That drama almost made her pull me out of Langdon, which would have made me happy before I met Marco. If she even suspected I might be getting in deep with the mystery that is Bethanie and her family, not to mention Cole, she'd probably begin to think Langdon was no better at keeping me out of trouble than my neighborhood school. She'd pull me out for real, before I had a chance to figure out why I'm pretty smart about a lot of things but such a screw-up at being a girlfriend.

The phone rings and Lana picks up. She listens to whoever is on the other end for about ten seconds, then says, "Not interested." She puts her hand over the mouthpiece and whispers to me, "Damn telemarketers."

I keep watching *Perry Mason,* expecting Lana to hang up on whoever is trying to sell her something like she usually does, but she keeps listening without saying a word for a minute. Then I guess her patience wears out.

"Do. Not. Ever. Call this house again or I will make you regret the day you found me or my phone number," she says before slamming down the phone.

Whoa. That's a little harsh for telemarketers. I bet they're bill collectors. Sometimes Lana can live a little beyond her means. Still, her threat sounded a bit too sinister even for the most annoying of bill collectors. The phone rings again, and this time Lana doesn't even find out who it is, just slams it right down the minute she picks it up.

"Pretty insistent telemarketers," I say. "I guess they really want to sell you something."

"Well, I'm not buying," she says, muting the commercials. "Did you ever talk to your friend about her boyfriend?"

"Yes."

"Did she take it well?"

"No."

"I feel like I'm questioning a perp. What's with the one-word answers?"

"Sorry. I've just been a little distracted."

Lana doesn't say anything, which is a cool thing about her. Maybe she learned it from interrogating bad guys, but she knows when to pull the words out of you and when to just let them come on their own. At the next commercial break, I mute *Perry Mason* again.

"What if she doesn't believe me, but I'm right?"

"Does it really matter if you're right? If that's the only reason you're telling her, let it go. If you're right and her not believing you has consequences beyond a broken heart, then you have to keep at it."

"Hard to do if she doesn't want to talk to me."

"You tend to be persistent. I'm sure you'll find a way." She picks up the remote, but doesn't turn up the volume. "Chanti, these consequences wouldn't be anything that will cause problems for you beyond a lost friendship, are they?"

Ah, she knows me too well.

"Nope, I just don't like the guy."

"If that's the only problem, it's best to stay out of it. She'll figure it out on her own."

I leave her to watch Perry get a confession out of the helpless loser on the witness stand so I can think through everything I know about my own case. Before I shift gears to Bethanie and Cole, I check the caller ID on the phone in my room without even really thinking about it. I guess I'm turning into Lana if my natural instincts tell me: (1) whoever just called is probably not a telemarketer or a bill collector, and (2) check the story. But I only confirm my first theory because the number is gone. In the time it took me to walk to my room, Lana has deleted it from the caller ID memory. So it was definitely not someone trying to sell her something or collect her money because she wouldn't have bothered to erase the number. Probably some crazy perp she put in jail is calling and making threats, which is too scary to think about, especially since they were able to find our unlisted phone number because that means they also know where we live.

So I think about my case instead, writing down clues on my mental whiteboard. I can't keep real notes lying around just like I can't keep a diary lying around—my mom snoops for a living. I'd like to think she doesn't snoop on me, but I'd rather not tempt her. Besides, I'm pretty sure I have a photographic memory, though I've never been tested for that. If I see it or hear it, I'm gonna remember it. Unless it's Lana telling me to do the laundry or Headmistress Smythe telling me to stay away from Marco. I *choose* to forget those things.

Notes on the Larsen Family

1. They keep lying about how they made their money in oil instead of the lottery.
2. The whole bunch, including the maid and driver, seems to be using an alias and pretending they're high society when they're so clearly not. Maybe they don't want long-lost family hitting them up for loans. But why let the world know they're rich at all? If you're hiding something, why not keep that on the down low, as well?
3. Bethanie's father seemed relieved Cole may have been only after money. What else do fathers worry about boys taking from their daughters? Okay, there's *that*. But if I were a dad, I wouldn't want some boy taking either That or money from my daughter.
4. What is up with that driver, anyway? Probably a family member who needed a job, and he helps them act out their high society charade, except he's really scary and would make any socialite run for a can of mace.

Notes on Cole

1. I'm convinced that robbery wasn't legit. He had to have been tailing Bethanie to know she'd be there on Freebie Friday, which means he'd been tailing her for a while. A guy in love enough to do that is crazy. I know crazy and he isn't it.
2. He dresses all GQ, picks fancy restaurants, but doesn't have a job or come from money. That spells gold digger to me.
3. He shows up just in time to rescue Bethanie from some thug waiting in her parking space, and with just a look, can scare this guy off. Cole is charming and cute, but not the least bit intimidating. So how does he stare down a thug and run off hungry people waiting for BOGO tamales?

4. And can I get a last name, please?

I figure that last one shouldn't be so hard to get if I can convince Bethanie to talk to me.

The next morning, I'm up early even though I got close to zero sleep thinking about my list of clues. The plan is to at least get a full name for Cole before the weekend is over. What kind of guy won't give his girl a last name? I'm also dying to know what they do all day when Bethanie is supposed to be in school and working for some charity afterward. I imagine it's a whole lot of shopping with her money, but even for Bethanie that has to get old after a while. Since Bethanie won't talk to me at school, I figure I'll go to her house. She could blow me off there, too, but I'd have her parents' backup because they want me to talk to her.

I do a repeat of last Sunday and get there when I know the Larsens are still in bed. Luckily Lana hadn't come in from last night's stakeout when I left, though I'll have to make up some story about where I've been so early on a Sunday morning if I don't make it back before she gets in. I can only hope her stakeout yielded a bunch of arrests that will keep her busy filing reports all morning.

After the two buses it takes me to get to Cherry Creek, I'm awake enough to realize I'm so early that it's almost rude. The frost has not even begun to melt off the grass and most driveways still have a newspaper lying at the end of them. I try to slow my gait, but it's so cold I really just want to be in someone's house with a cup of coffee warming my hands. Just as I round the curve to Bethanie's street, I see a car turning off, it heading toward me. A few seconds later, another car turns off and heads the same way the first car does. That guy is going to get so busted for having an obstructed view if a cop sees him—he didn't scrape the frost off the windows and I'm pretty sure he can't see much. He must be in one hell of a hurry to get to work if he couldn't bother to scrape off more than a peephole, though I doubt anyone in this neighborhood works weekends.

The fact that at least two people on Bethanie's street are awake makes me think I'm not being so rude after all, and when I get to her house, I see Mr. Larsen pulling out of the driveway. He waves to me and keeps on driving. Maybe I have the rich and idle all wrong and they aren't as idle as I think. That must mean Bethanie and her mother are awake, too. When I have to ring the bell about ten times, I realize that isn't the case.

"Are you insane?" Bethanie says when the door finally opens.

"No, but since I need to talk to you and you're barely in school these days—and you avoid me when you are—I figured I'd come here when I knew you'd be home."

"Go home," she says, actually closing the door in my face, but not before I put my hand up to stop it.

"You can't give me a few minutes?"

"For what?"

"To apologize."

Now she seems interested. Enough to invite me in and fix me a cup of instant coffee when I ask for something to help me warm up. Instant coffee is just wrong on so many levels, but I'm freezing so I relax my standards.

"So you want to apologize for thinking my boyfriend is a gold digger out to rob me blind?"

"I could have been more receptive about a relationship that is obviously making you so happy," I say, really trying not to lie while still regaining her confidence. It works, because she seems to interpret it as an apology.

"Good, because I want your opinion about something," she says, joining me at the breakfast bar with her own cup of bad coffee. "How do you get a guy to be interested?"

"If I knew the answer to that I'd be home a lot less often on weekends."

"You got Marco's interest."

"Yeah, but I don't know how to hold on to it." Or I'm not willing to—I haven't yet decided exactly what my problem is when it comes to Marco.

"Not me. I wouldn't have that problem if I had the guy I wanted, and I sure wouldn't let my parents keep us apart."

"Wait—why are you even asking? Is there someone else besides Cole?" I say, hoping I don't sound too excited about that.

"No, of course not. I'm talking about Cole."

"It seems like you've already got him pretty interested. He wants to be with you practically 24/7 as it is."

"That's just it. All the time we've spent together, we have never even kissed."

I must look incredulous to her, because I am.

"See, you didn't know what you were talking about, suggesting statutory . . . I can't even say it. That's the farthest thing from where Cole and I are."

Wow, neither of us are in danger of getting jobs as romance advice columnists. Bethanie doesn't know how to get the boy she wants, and I don't know what to do with the boy I have.

"Okay, so what do you do all that time when you're skipping class?"

"Drive around, get something to eat, see movies, go to the museum. A couple of times we went to bet on the dogs."

"Preppie Cole doesn't seem the dog track type."

"He must have realized that, too, because both times we only stayed a few minutes, just walked around and never even placed a bet. He said I was underage, and he wouldn't place one for me. I swear, I might as well be hanging out with my parents."

Oh, *now* he thinks she's underage. And somehow I can't imagine her parents at a museum.

"That's kind of weird," I say. "I mean, a guy who wants to

be with you but not be *with* you. Isn't that what they're all trying to get every second of the day?"

"I thought so. But he *is* a gentleman. I guess I should appreciate that."

This revelation just puts a whole new kink in the mystery. I still think Cole wants her money, but why not get the girl, too? Especially when Bethanie seems more than a little interested in moving the relationship in that direction.

"Good, I'm glad to see you two girls talking again, even if it's at a god-awful hour," Mrs. Larsen says, coming into the kitchen. "Where's your father?"

"How should I know?" Bethanie says with a whole lot of attitude.

"The only reason I'm up this early is because he woke me when he got out of bed. He must be around here somewhere," Mrs. Larsen says.

"I saw him leaving this morning; that's why I figured y'all were up when I rang the bell," I say.

"Where was he going?" asks Mrs. Larsen.

"I didn't talk to him. I just saw him pulling out of your garage. Seemed like he was in a hurry, just like the other two cars I saw turning off your street just before he left."

Mrs. Larsen goes over to a window that looks onto the backyard, not the front of the house, like she thinks I'm lying and her husband is really back there.

"Have you seen Tiny?" she asks, still scanning the backyard like Tiny might be hiding back there along with Mr. Larsen.

"No, Mom. Um, Chanti and I were trying to have a conversation."

"Mr. Larsen was driving himself," I offer in the way of Tiny's whereabouts.

"What? Oh, right. Mr. Larsen usually drives himself. Not to worry," she says as though I might, although she looks plenty worried herself. "I don't want to interrupt you girls, especially if Chantal is trying to talk some sense into you."

"Talk some sense into me?"

"Your father don't like this person—Cole—you've been hanging out with."

"I never told you his name," Bethanie says, looking at me like she wants to kill me. "You told them. You've been talking to *them*?"

Before I can salvage the situation, Mrs. Larsen says, "She agrees with us that this Cole is up to no good. I think . . ."

Bethanie doesn't wait to hear what her mother thinks. She leaves the kitchen, not even bothering to pick up her bar stool when she knocks it over getting up so fast. I'm pretty sure she'll never trust me again, and I wouldn't blame her.

Chapter 11

I manage to get home and put my pajamas back on just minutes before Lana walks in the door. For extra measure, I smash my hair in a little on the side, but in case she thinks I look a bit too wide-eyed for nine on a Sunday morning, I make sure I have a pot of *real* coffee brewing and my homework spread out on the kitchen table.

"You're up early," she says when she walks into the kitchen, just like I expected her to.

"I was kind of slack about homework this weekend and couldn't sleep worrying about it, so I figured I might as well get up and do it. Want some coffee?"

"It smells good, but I need to sleep for about two days first."

Excellent—suspicion avoided.

When the phone rings, Lana says, "Who could be calling this early?"

I jump to answer it because I suspect it could only be Bethanie to curse me out for my traitorous ways. I'm relieved when I see the caller ID.

"Someone from Atlanta."

"Don't answer it," Lana says—too late because I pick up on the third ring. The way she's looking at me you'd think I might contract the plague from whoever is on the other end of the line.

"Hello?"

"I'm sorry to call so early on Sunday, but I'd like to speak to Lana Evans please," says the Southern-accented woman.

"Mrs. Larsen? Why do you want to speak to my mother?"

"This is Detective Sanders of the Atlanta Police Department," the woman says, sounding so much like Bethanie's mother I think she might be lying, but I hand the phone to Lana anyway.

"Someone claiming to be from the Atlanta PD."

Lana looks about ten shades of relieved. After I hand her the phone, the doorbell rings and I open the door to find Bethanie standing there. She must have been in a hurry to see me because she's dressed the same way she was when I left her house—flannel sleep pants, a long-sleeved T-shirt and Mukluks. Very un-Bethanie.

"I figured you'd never want to talk to me again," I say.

"I didn't, but I thought of a way for you to redeem yourself. You gonna let me in? It's cold out here."

I can hear Lana on the phone, but I can't risk her call ending and finding Bethanie here. She'd start interrogating me right away: Why is that girl here on a Sunday morning? Why did you think her mother would be calling looking for me?

"No, let's go sit in your car. My mom's in a mood," I say, grabbing a coat to put on over my pj's.

"What's with the pajamas and the bed head?" Bethanie asks. "You were wearing lip gloss and earrings an hour ago."

"Long story, not at all interesting. Besides, I think you're the one with some explaining to do," I say, pointing out her outfit in case she's delirious and doesn't realize she left the house in her pajamas. As fashion-challenged as I am, I'd never do that.

Once we're in her car, she says, "I need a favor. It's your

chance to prove you're a real friend and not a snitch. I want you to cover for me this weekend, tell my parents I'm staying with you."

"So you can hang out with Cole?"

She doesn't respond, which is really an answer. Just then, Tasha comes out of her house to get the paper. I'm hoping she'll go right back inside, but no, Tasha is just that nosy.

"Who is that?" Bethanie asks.

"A friend. She'll just say hi and go back inside," I say, rolling down the window. "Hey, girl, what's up?"

"What's up with you? You're the one sitting out here in this nice car," Tasha says, leaning in to get a look at the driver.

"This is—"

"I'm her friend from school," Bethanie says, interrupting me. "We have something kind of major going on. You mind?"

Bethanie rolls my window back up before Tasha can even back away. I give Tasha a look that I hope says *I'm sorry*, but she looks too through with me. I'll have to do some damage control later. I can see why Bethanie has no friends but me.

"Rude much?"

"The fewer people in my business, the better. So . . . will you do it?"

"But won't you be with him anyway without me lying for you?"

"Not overnight."

"What happened in the hour since I last saw you? I thought he was such a gentleman."

"Cole called me right after you left. I told him how impossible my parents are being about him. About everything."

"What else are they upset about?" I know something else is going on in the Larsen household. When her parents talked to me about helping them do an intervention, they almost seemed happy Cole was after their money, a response I still haven't figured out.

"They want to put me on lockdown even more than ever."

"Because of Cole?"

"Cole . . . everything."

"Can't say I'd blame them. I mean, they *are* parents. It's kind of their job to keep you from getting in so deep with a guy you just met."

"It's just like *Romeo and Juliet*, the way they want to keep us apart."

A squad car goes running hot down Center Street, so I wait for it to pass before I tell Bethanie what I think, as nicely as possible, of course, because she needs to hear it clearly.

"This is nothing like *Romeo and Juliet*. In order for them to have a feud, their families had to know one another. You don't know Cole's parents; you don't even know his last name. And now you're having a sleepover with the guy?"

"You don't have a romantic bone in your body, Chanti. That's why you can't win Marco back."

"I can't win Marco back because he respects his parents and they think I might get him killed. I don't blame them, either, since history proves they have a point," I say, without adding that I'm actually relieved they're giving me an excuse not to advance past a first kiss with Marco. "This is not about romance."

"Maybe not completely. Cole suggested I stay with him over the weekend when we talked this morning. He was so sweet. He said he just feels this need to protect me."

"From what—your parents? Because I'm pretty sure it should be the other way around," I say, forgetting I'm supposed to be trying to win back her trust.

"Maybe *protect* was the wrong word, but I know what he meant. You don't know everything about me, Chanti."

That's an understatement. I'm beginning to think I don't know anything about Bethanie. "And Cole knows more than I do?"

"Look, I really like him no matter what the rest of you think, and I know he cares about me. He always seems so sad when we have to separate and I have to go home. I figure if we can have a couple of days together, uninterrupted by parental drama, then maybe he'll come around and start acting like my boyfriend and not my brother."

I'm trying to approach my next question in a way that doesn't sound like some public service announcement, but there's really no way around it, so I just say it.

"Bethanie, do your parents hit you or something?"

"What?" she says, then breaks out laughing. Not the response I was expecting. "Is that what you think is going on? And you look so serious, too. You better not quit your day job if that's what your detective skills are telling you."

"Well, you're always so cryptic, and now Cole is talking about protecting you from something you can tell him about but not me."

"I told you he just used the wrong word. Believe me, my secrets are nowhere near as dark as you think."

"You're going to find a way to do this with or without my help, aren't you?"

"Yes. But this way is easiest. My parents trust you."

Great. Way to make me feel better about going along with this plan. But Bethanie seems to be going off the rails over this guy, and if I can't stop her and her parents can't, either, I figure it's smart to keep her trust and make sure I at least know what she's up to.

"Speaking of parents," I say, remembering the cop who just called Lana, "is your mother from Georgia—Atlanta maybe?"

When I say this, you'd have thought I just asked Bethanie for her left kidney. She looks terrified and doesn't say anything, just stares straight ahead and grips the steering wheel like she expects to be sucked right out of the car and has to hold on for dear life.

Finally she says, "Why do you ask that?"

"You never talk about where you're from or anything about your family, so I was just wondering. . . ."

"Are you doing that whole girl-detective thing on me again?"

"No," I say, hoping my lie isn't obvious. "But you want to be friends, want me to lie to your parents, and you can't even tell me something like where you're from?"

"I barely know anything about your mother, and you never talk about your father."

"My father left the scene about the time I became a zygote; for all I know, he's not even walking the planet anymore. And you can come inside right now if you want to meet my mom," I say, hoping she won't call my bluff. I don't need any questions from Lana about Bethanie.

"What made you think my mother is from Atlanta?"

"A friend of my mom from Atlanta just called—and she sounds a lot like your mother."

This seems to be a good answer because she relaxes, letting go of the steering wheel and looking at me again.

"Look, will you just do this for me or not?"

"I'll do it, but only if you give me Cole's address."

"Why? I thought you said he was a gold digger, not a kidnapper."

"I don't think he's a kidnapper, but I at least need to know where you'll be if I'm going to lie for you."

"I don't know his address."

"Where do y'all go if you've never been to his place?"

"I told you—restaurants, museums, movies. I'll find out and give it to you."

"Will you be in school this week?"

"Of course. I have to sell the whole story to my parents, right? Chanti is showing me the error of my ways, no more skipping school, no more Cole, yada yada."

After I get out of her car and she drives away, I turn to the house and see Lana watching me through the blinds. I'm on a roll with the lies today; let's see what I can come up with for Lana.

"There's that big BMW again," she says.

"That was the friend I was telling you about. She came to talk to me about the boy."

"So she's come around to what you've been telling her?"

"Something like that."

"Why couldn't you invite her in instead of sitting in her car like you were making a drug deal?"

Only a mother who's a vice cop would ever think up that analogy. Which actually gives me my cover story, which is not really a story at all.

"You were on the phone talking police stuff. And you left your gun and badge right there on the table when you came in this morning. I didn't want to have to explain that to her."

"Wow, I really must be tired to have done that. Good save."

Most times the truth works a whole lot better than a lie. I just have to hope the one Bethanie and I are planning to tell this weekend doesn't backfire on me.

Chapter 12

Over breakfast the next morning, I ask Lana if her detective skills are so amazing that people in Atlanta are calling for advice.

"About that," she says, "how much of a problem would it be for you to miss a couple days of school this week?"

"Missing school is never a problem," I say, especially when you think your quasi-boyfriend may have dumped you and you have to steer clear of him in the halls and cafeteria so you can avoid having that confirmed.

"How about exams, papers?"

"No—why?"

"I need to go to Atlanta for a long weekend. There's a big case they're working that has connections to Denver and my CO offered my help to the police department down there."

"Cool. Friday's a teacher work day, anyway."

"We'll take a late flight Wednesday and fly back Sunday."

Then I remember the Cole case and how my very few leads will go completely cold by Sunday. "Wait—you want me to go with you? I've got stuff to do here."

"You just said it wasn't a problem, and I quote: 'Cool. Friday's a teacher work day, anyway.'"

"I forgot about some commitments I have."

Lana laughs at this. "What commitments could you have other than school? You can't stay here by yourself."

"Why not? You're always saying I'm mature for my age."

"You are, but that doesn't change the fact you're fifteen and I could be arrested for leaving you alone for four days."

"I'll be sixteen soon and I stay overnight by myself all the time when you're on stakeout. What's the difference?"

"The difference is eight hours versus four days. The difference is I'll be fourteen hundred miles away, not ten. Plus it will be a good chance to see your grandparents."

I quietly sulk, trying to think up a way out of this trip.

"Look, Chanti, Atlanta is the last place I want to be right now, believe me."

I actually do believe her since she keeps avoiding all phone calls with a 404 area code lately. But clearly she's going there anyway, since her *take no crap* face has replaced her *let's negotiate* face. That doesn't keep me from trying.

"I just remembered I *do* have something going on at school. I definitely need to be there Thursday."

"I'll write a note for your teachers."

"So when you asked if school would be a problem, that was just a hypothetical."

She raises her eyebrow at me, and I know I'm testing her limits now, but I'm not there yet.

"What if I promise not to go anywhere but school and back, and stay in the house all weekend?"

"No."

"Why can't I just stay at Tasha's house? I've done that before when you had to travel."

"Because this is different. I want you with me."

"Is it about that perp who's been calling the house?"

"A perp's been calling? How . . . you should have told me. What did he say?"

"I don't know, I haven't talked to him. The one you

warned not to ever call here again. You said it was a telemarketer, but I know it's someone more serious than that."

"That's not your business. And I don't need a reason why you're coming with me other than I'm your mother and I said so."

Now she's wearing her *I brought you into this world and I can take you out* face, and I know better than to mess with her when she shows that one. I can't do anything but leave for school.

I was wrong when I thought my agreement to Bethanie's plan was a détente in our mini-war. This is what I'm thinking while I try to stay awake in Western Civ, which explains the war reference. It's sixth period and Bethanie has managed to avoid me all day, just like I've been doing with Marco, though I'm pretty sure he hasn't been looking for me, either. This whole avoidance thing is feeling just like a rerun of last week, and that episode was lame enough without having to repeat it. I'm determined to set them both straight before last bell. We're all adults here, mostly, and I'd think we could discuss our problems rather than running the silent treatment. First stop—Marco.

I corner him outside the door of his seventh period class.

"Can we talk for a second?"

"I'm running late," he says.

"We still have four minutes to bell. It just felt weird the way we left it last week, Marco. I'd rather know what's going on instead of wondering."

He's looking over my head at something extremely interesting down the hall, but when I look behind me, there's just the usual sea of kids trying to get to class, steal a few bites from their locker food stash, or rehash the party they went to over the weekend. Clearly he has something to say that he *really* doesn't want to. I decide to make it easy for him.

"I'm a big girl. Whatever you need to say, say it."

"It's just I don't get what's going on with you. I mean, I thought you liked me. . . ."

I start to say that he's right, I way more than like him, but he puts up his hand so I won't stop him.

"But you keep doing stuff that makes it so my parents will stop me from seeing you. I won't lie to them. Most kids might, but I won't. Even when I'm willing to break the rules a little, you don't seem interested. And a hallway romance is just not enough for me, not when I'm crazy about you."

Okay, that last part is excellent news. I wish I could kiss him right here in the hall, but Smythe is on monitor duty.

"If you're crazy about me, that means you have to be crazy about who I am and what I do."

"Chanti, do you not realize that just a couple of weeks ago, because you were playing mini-cop, I was wrestling away a gun from a guy who was about to kill us? If it had gone the other way, we wouldn't be having this conversation."

"But here we are."

"This is not a joke. I would think you'd stay as far away from trouble as you could seeing how we already stared Death down once. But now you're talking about Bethanie's guy being some kind of stalker and how you have to investigate him."

"Wouldn't you want to save a friend from a potential stalker?"

"How can the guy be a stalker if they've been out on a date? I was there, remember? Oh, wait. Maybe you don't because you were as into that Cole guy as Bethanie was."

"I explained that, Marco. It was strictly a business interest."

"See, that's the problem. Bethanie and her date are *not* your business. Detective work is not your business, either, even if you've watched a few too many episodes of *CSI* and think it is."

"But she's my friend."

"She's my friend, too, and it seems to me the guy makes her happy. That's all I wanted—a chance to make you happy," Marco says, moving in close to whisper his last words in my ear.

"I . . . Oh, wow, believe me, you make me happy," I say, his proximity making it very hard for me to sound coherent. But he fixes that by stepping back suddenly and looking me in the eyes and not in a dreamy sort of way.

"And even if I thought she was in some kind of real danger, I'd realize I don't have the skills to help and I'd call the police, or tell her parents, or go to Smythe over there for help. I'd do what I needed to do to keep us from being over."

The bell rings, and I don't feel at all saved by it.

"I need to get to class," he says, turning to leave.

"Wait, Marco. I have to go out of town in a couple of days and I don't want to be wondering about us."

"A break would be good. You can figure out if you'd rather play detective or be with me."

After that emotional smack-down, I don't even bother looking for Bethanie, and spend all of seventh period trying not to cry onto my calculus textbook.

I wake up Tuesday and feign illness because I can't find the energy to go to school and pretend Marco didn't just break my heart. That would involve doing the opposite of avoidance. I'd have to run into him practically everywhere, smiling like yesterday was nothing but a thing. Lana buys into it and calls the school to tell them I'm sick because her main concern is me being well enough to travel. I took the opportunity to state my case about staying home while she's in Atlanta since I'm sick, but she wasn't hearing it.

Bored out of my mind, I've spent the day online trying to find what I can about the Larsens, and there is absolutely no information. There is pretty much nothing I can't find on the

Web—I've even helped Lana on some searches for cases that I probably shouldn't have known a thing about—but it's like the Larsens don't even exist, whether I search in Denver or Atlanta.

That's when it occurs to me that I should look at this trip a whole different way. For one thing, it'll take my mind off Marco. Okay, it won't, but at least it'll give me something else to think about. After my last conversation with Bethanie, I don't doubt that whatever her family is running from, it's in Atlanta. Maybe while I'm there, I can check out some sources you can't find online. Not that I have any, but Lana does. Somehow I'll have to get her help without her knowing it. I start by undoing all the snark I've given her the past couple of days.

"I made dinner," I say as soon as she gets home.

"Really? Are you feeling better?"

"Lots. Sorry I've been such a pain. Maybe it was because I was sick."

"You started being a pain before you got sick, but I forgive you."

"Marco and I broke up," I say, making sure I'm taking bowls out of the cabinet as I do so she can't see my face. She'll start reading my expression and ask what else is going on besides my breakup.

"Oh, Chanti, I'm sorry. Is that why you've been out of sorts?"

"Maybe. I'm still trying to get used to the idea."

"Want to talk about it?"

"No, it's okay. We hadn't really been together very long, so I'm good," I say, because saying it might convince me it's true. "Let's talk about something else."

I ladle chili into the bowls and take the corn bread out of the oven, a little proud of what I can do with some Jiffy mix, a pound of ground beef, and a can of chili starter. When I put the food on the table, along with a big salad, I can tell Lana is impressed. Operation Unsnark is moving right along.

"So what's up with this new case? You haven't told me much."

I think she's been waiting since that phone call from the Atlanta PD to tell me, because she just lights up about it.

"It's huge. The US Marshals Service is involved. It could be so great for my career."

That means it might help her get into Homicide Division. Lana loves Vice, but Homicide is like the Holy Grail for cops.

"US Marshals—that *is* big-time. I guess that makes sense if he's a fugitive. That means he was in the Witness Security Program, right?"

"That's my girl!"

My mother loves it when I know stuff like that. I'm totally getting on her good side now.

"So how much can you tell me?"

"You know this is for your ears only—"

"When do I ever tell anything?" I'm almost insulted. Even Lana doesn't guard her cases or the fact that she's an undercover cop better than I do.

"A suspect who turned state's witness in a trial of a crime family's boss has disappeared. They think he might be here. And I'm going to find him."

Chapter 13

On the plane's approach over Atlanta, I'm always amazed by how many trees there are. When you see trees in Denver, you know someone planted them because it's mostly plains and desert. Flying over Atlanta, you can tell the trees were here first and someone planted the city around them, instead of the other way around. The whole flight, I try to think up a scheme to get Lana to help me with the Cole case without her realizing I was even working a case, but come up with nothing. Not that I'd have been able to implement the scheme right away—Lana is a nervous flier so she took a Xanax the second we stepped onto the plane. She's been knocked out ever since. I just keep mentally running through everything I've ever learned about Bethanie's family so I'd at least have an idea of what to look for in what I'm certain is their hometown.

After we land, I turn on my phone and see Bethanie has blown it up with texts asking where I am and why I haven't been in school all week. She's got a nerve, seeing how she's been ditching half her classes for nearly two weeks now. It's close to midnight here because we took a late flight out, but it's not quite ten there, so I give her a call while Lana watches for our bags on the baggage carousel.

"Where've you been?" Bethanie demands as soon as she hears my voice. "I've called and texted you all day."

"So you can go AWOL and not say a thing, but I have to report in to you?"

"I need to make sure you're still giving me my cover story this weekend. I'm making plans."

"To do what?"

"It's private. But are you still going to do it?"

I gesture to Lana that I'm moving to a bank of chairs across from the carousel, and once she's out of hearing range, I answer Bethanie. "When I get Cole's address."

"I'll get it soon."

"Text me as soon as you get it and you have a deal. I won't be at school the rest of the week."

"You haven't been in school this week at all."

"I was there Monday. Maybe *you* weren't there to see me. I think Marco broke up with me. I couldn't deal with seeing him, so I faked sick yesterday."

"You *think* he broke up with you? What did he say?"

I remembered it word for word because I've been replaying it a hundred times a day hoping I misinterpreted it. Maybe Bethanie can give me an objective opinion.

"He said I should use the break to figure out if I'd rather play detective or be with him."

"What did he mean about you playing detective?"

Oops. The suspicion enters her voice instantly.

"He still hasn't gotten over that whole burglary thing last month."

"And what break are you talking about?"

"Yeah, that's the thing I was going to tell you about. Make sure you give your mom my cell if she wants to check up on you this weekend. I'm not in Denver, and won't be back until Sunday."

"You should have told me you wouldn't be here. I'd have found someone else to be my cover."

"Who else would do it?" I ask, since we both know I'm her only friend besides Marco, and he won't lie for her.

"Well, you just should have told me, that's all. Where are you, anyway?"

Here goes.

"Atlanta. I'm at the airport now."

Silence on the other end for a few seconds, then, "Why would you be there, all out of the blue and everything?"

"Just something I have to take care of," I say, nodding at Lana when she motions to me that she has our luggage. "Bethanie, I have to go now."

"Hold up a minute. Unless you've suddenly become the president, how do you get to just jump on a plane to take care of something on the other side of the country?"

"You sound so suspicious. I'm just here visiting my grandparents for a few days. I'm with my mother. What's your deal, anyway?" I ask, although I know exactly what her deal is.

"It's just you never told me you had family there. Are they okay? I mean, for you to just take off, missing class and everything. . . ."

"Everything is great. Just something we needed to do, that's all."

"All right, that's cool. Just don't screw this weekend up for me, okay?"

"Don't forget to let me know where you'll be. I need that address or I won't lie for you."

"You'll get it," she says, and doesn't bother to say good-bye.

My favorite thing about visiting my grandparents, besides seeing them, is how nothing ever changes. I know before I walk in the door that the furniture will be in the same place it was the last time I was here. There will be Brach's caramels in the candy bowl on the coffee table, and a copy of *TV*

Guide even though they have cable and can check the on-screen guide. I know after we do all of our hugging, we'll go into the kitchen where my grandmother will have a fresh pot of coffee waiting because she somehow knows the exact time we'll show up at her door. We always drive on our summer visits since Lana hates to fly, and Grandma always can time when we're going to pull into her driveway. Taking the plane this time, then renting a car at the airport, didn't throw off her timing a bit. With all the changes I've been through lately—new school, new boyfriend who became my ex overnight, getting arrested—I could really use a few days of everything being the same.

I called the whole reunion right. The house is the exact same as far as I can tell, and even though it's close to one in the morning, I can smell fresh-brewed coffee. My grandmother is surprised when I ask for a cup.

"You let her drink coffee now, Lana? You know that'll stunt her growth."

"That's just an old wives' tale, Mama. Besides, she's almost sixteen. She's pretty much done growing."

Though I'd be good if my hips stopped growing, I hope Lana is wrong because I wouldn't mind adding another letter to my bra size. Right now, with all the stress from almost going to jail, Marco dropping me, and Bethanie dating a con artist, the size matches my grades at school—A on the cusp of becoming a B. Not the strongest prospects for getting into the best colleges or out of a padded bra. It wouldn't rock my world if it doesn't happen (the bra thing, not the college thing—that's a must) but I change my mind on the coffee, just in case.

"Guess who called here the other day?" my grandfather says to Lana, who I suspect doesn't have to guess because her face tenses up right away. "It was like talking to a ghost."

"Did he know you were coming?" my grandmother asks. "It's some coincidence if not."

"Look, Mama, it's been a long day, and we're tired," Lana says, getting up from the table. "I've got an early day at the police department tomorrow, so I'd better get some sleep. Let's take our bags upstairs, Chanti."

I want to tell her I'm too wired to go to sleep, but it's clear Lana doesn't want to talk about the ghost who seemed to know she'd be in town this weekend. Since I'm trying to stay on her good side so she can unwittingly help me get information on Bethanie's family and on who Cole really is, I kiss my grandparents good night and grab our bags.

Lana and I always share her old bedroom when we visit. It looks the same as the day she left, and it always freaks me out when I see the posters of Will Smith when he was still the Fresh Prince and a really young Usher. Before I was even born, she was crushing on the same guys I like now. I guess that's what happens when your mom is just sixteen years older than you and has great taste in men who still look good even though they're old.

Her twin beds still wear the same comforters she picked out just before she got pregnant with me. They look girlier than anything I would have chosen and nothing like the Lana I know, even from my earliest memory of her. Every time I see this room, I imagine what it must have been like to lie on the frilly pink bed, stare at Usher and Will, and absorb the news delivered by the pregnancy stick. Is that the moment she stopped being girly? Did she have to grow up on the spot, or did that come after she'd been a mom a few months and realized she couldn't be a girl and raise a girl at the same time?

I never think about that until I come here and hang out in her old bedroom, and then I think of a million things to ask Lana that I never do. Did she have to skip her prom because they didn't make maternity prom dresses? How silly did the girls sound at school talking about makeup and hairstyles when she'd been up all night cramming for a midterm and dealing with a screaming kid? She always says I was a good baby, but I doubt it. Without even trying, I probably started causing trouble in the womb.

I'm sure I made dating difficult. I'm guessing the ghost who called earlier is Lana's boyfriend from college, the one she was crazy about who told her things could get serious between them. Well, until he found out five-year-old me was living with my grandparents in the frilly pink room only until Lana finished college, not indefinitely.

Lana must have lied to Grandma about being tired because she's not going to sleep. She has spread all her case files out on the bed and is just staring at everything. It looks like she's zoned out, but that's the way Lana tries to put the clues together. I move over to her twin bed, hoping she's so focused on the files that she doesn't notice I'm looking at them, too. No such luck. She starts gathering up all the papers and closes the folder I was looking at. But not before I caught a glimpse of something that gives me a serious WTF moment.

"What's the deal with the informant? Why do they think he's in Denver?" I ask.

"It's pretty cool how they figured that out. The guy is a compulsive gambler and the marshals figured he couldn't stop, even on the run. So they started checking security camera tape in casinos, racetracks, off-track betting locations, and they found him."

"Oh snap," I say. My WTF moment just grew exponentially more serious.

"What?"

"Nothing. I just think this sounds like something I saw in a movie last week."

"It really does," Lana says, buying my explanation why I probably look just a little freaked out. "He started at Alabama racetracks, Mississippi riverboat casinos, and kept moving west until he dropped off the radar in New Mexico at an Indian casino. They figured he might show up next at one of the mountain casinos back home, but he just disappeared."

"They think the people he was supposed to testify against found him before they did?"

"Not yet, but they're probably close enough to scare the witness underground. If the defendant finds him first, that would blow the prosecution's whole case, which was built on the guy's testimony. Not to mention probably get him killed. So I'm here to learn as much as I can about the case so I can go home and help marshals in the Denver office find him."

"But I thought he was at the mountain casinos."

"You can't stay hidden up in those small towns where everyone knows each other. If he's gambling up there, he's probably living in Denver where he can disappear a little easier. The feds might have all the high-tech surveillance in the world, but they just don't know a city the way a city cop knows it."

This gets Lana started on her beef with the feds. If you watch any cop show often enough, there will be a story line where local law enforcement gets into a whole jurisdiction fight with the federal agencies, usually the FBI. That's one cliché Hollywood gets right. From my experience (by way of Lana's experience), there isn't much love between the locals and the feds. If you know any cops who ever had to work a case the feds were also looking at, you've heard the story. I've heard it more than once from Lana, and I must not have been as wired as I thought because I fall asleep on her explaining how the feds don't know the streets or the informants like a vice cop does. I guess being drop-dead tired even trumps fear, because I'm pretty sure I recognized a guy in one of those pictures before Lana put away her files. My last thought before I start drooling on the pillow is that my friend might be crushing on a fugitive.

Chapter 14

In the light of morning, I'm thinking my eyes were playing tricks on me last night, or I just didn't have enough time to really see the photo before Lana closed her folder. It sounds crazy, but add what I thought I saw to Cole's joking about his gambling habit over dinner and Bethanie's reporting that he keeps taking her to dog tracks, and maybe it isn't so crazy. If it was Cole in that photo, then it's probably no coincidence that he's found his way to Bethanie. Well, I already knew he was stalking her; this just confirms I'm right. Now the question is why.

After Lana leaves for the police department the next morning, I stay in my room checking county and city property records Web sites hoping to find information on the Larsens. That's a lot of Web sites because there are a ton of cities and counties in the metro area. Everybody within a thirty-mile radius of Atlanta says they're from here, even if their address says differently. Since I'm only working on a hunch that the Larsens are from around Atlanta, I have to check them all. So far, I get nothing on their names, but that only means I haven't looked widely enough or they never owned property, which seems pretty unlikely for people with Powerball money.

I decide to call Bethanie to see if she has Cole's address for me yet and, oh yeah, find out if he's on the run from the law. But first I need to butter her up into thinking I support this crazy plan of spending the weekend with him. If I can manage that, I might be able to get some information out of her about her family.

"Can you ever call or visit someone at a decent hour?" Bethanie says, sounding like she just woke up.

"Sorry, I keep forgetting I'm two hours ahead. But it's six there; you should be getting up for school, anyway."

"I'm thinking of skipping."

"Remember you have to keep the charade going for your parents, right? Smythe will call home if you don't show, and she might be ready to kick you out of Langdon if you keep it up. It's just one more day and then you'll be hanging with Cole."

"I suppose that's true. Why are you suddenly all Miss Supportive?" she says, sounding more awake and a little suspicious.

"Because I've been thinking about what you said. I probably am just jealous of you since Marco dumped me."

"So you're sure it's over between you?"

"Pretty much," I say, even though I haven't talked to Marco since that hallway conversation. But he made it pretty clear—I just didn't want to believe it at the time.

"That's too bad. Maybe you guys can still work it out."

"Maybe, but for now I have to live vicariously through you and Cole. Did you get his address yet?"

"Yeah, I'm at his place now. I'll text it to you when I hang up."

"What's it like?"

I imagine Cole lives on a polo field, probably because when I first met him, I thought he might be a Ralph Lauren model who got his clothes on employee discount because that's all he ever wears. And maybe Hilfiger when he's slumming.

"Nothing special," Bethanie says.

"Really?"

"Don't get excited, Chanti. It isn't that he's broke. It's just temp housing—you know, one of those executive apartments until he decides whether he's staying in Denver. Hopefully I'll be influencing that decision."

Oh, there are so many tangents I could go off on after that statement, but I stay focused.

"So what's the big plan?" I ask.

She goes silent for a second.

"Still there?"

"Yeah. I'm just bummed because there *is* no big plan. I thought since he suggested I spend the weekend with him, we'd be doing something more than the usual. Now it sounds like more of the same, except I'll get to hang at his place and eat pizza."

"Well, that leaves a lot of time for romance, if you know what I mean."

"I can still hold out hope for that, but he hasn't even kissed me yet."

"Seriously?" It's killing me that I can't figure this guy out. What kind of guy wants to get his girl alone for three days and just order pizza?

"The most exciting thing we ever do is play poker. Now I wish I'd never taught him how."

"You taught him?" This makes me all kinds of relieved. Lana's fugitive would already know how to play poker.

"We needed something to kill all the time we *don't* spend making out. Maybe I should teach him strip poker, but I'd have to throw a lot of games since he isn't very good. I think that's the only way I'll get him to notice I have other assets."

"Other assets?" A-ha! So I was right about that part. Cole

really is trying to get Bethanie's money. Maybe she's figured it out, too.

"He thinks I'm wasting my brain."

"How's that?"

"He says I put up all these fake personas. Homegirl who doesn't have interest in good grades. Rich, vacuous diva. I made the mistake of telling him I've got a one hundred fifty-nine IQ and he just won't—"

"Wow, I thought I was smart. You beat me out by a few points. He's right—you definitely hide that."

"You saying I'm not too bright?"

"Obviously you're smart. So why do you get grades that are just good enough to stay in Langdon, and talk about Fashion Week and shopping like they're critical to achieving world peace?"

"Maybe I was tired of being the human calculator. I wanted to be like other girls—talk about clothes, go to parties, have a boyfriend."

"And you never did those things before because you were a . . . human calculator?" I don't know what exactly she means by that, but I'm pretty sure there's a clue in there somewhere.

"Math. That's my thing. I'm brilliant at it, according to my teachers. Before Langdon, back at my old school, I was taking college level courses starting in eighth grade. But the minute people find out, there goes all the fun."

"So why did you tell him about it?"

"I didn't. He figured it out when I kept beating him in poker. Math helps you figure out the odds. I guess a lot of the professional poker players are math geniuses or something."

"There are worse things you could be than a math genius. You could probably get a full scholarship to MIT or Cal Tech."

"I don't care about that right now. What I care about this weekend is making sure I won't be the only virgin in twelfth grade next year, and I can't even get a kiss."

"I'm pretty sure you won't be the only one," I say, 'cause there will at least be me in the club, especially after Marco just dumped me. And I'm pretty sure half the girls who claim to have done it, haven't.

"I gotta get ready for school. My parents think I'm going to your house after class tomorrow, so they'll probably call tomorrow night."

"What if they want to talk to my mother?"

"They won't. They think you walk on water and will show me the error of my ways. But if they do, just fake it. It isn't like they know her voice."

After she hangs up, I realize I didn't get much information about her family, except for that human calculator thing. When my phone rings, I hope it might be Marco but I'm sure it's Bethanie with some instruction she forgot to tell me on how I'm supposed to help her lie, so I'm surprised when I hear MJ's voice.

"I haven't seen you around for a couple of days and wondered what's up," MJ says, not wasting time on subtleties, like a greeting.

"MJ, is that you?"

"24/7/365. Look, we haven't talked since that morning in front of the bodega—"

"And you were wondering if I've been so quiet because I've been looking into what you know about the robbery, who Eddie is and how he plays into it, right?"

"Something like that," MJ says, sounding a little peeved that I've read her so well.

"As interested as I am in learning what you know, I'm working on something else right now that needs my full attention."

"Like an investigation?"

"Nothing you'd be interested in," I say, not ready to share my theories on Cole. At this point, it's all a hunch, a crazy-sounding one that Bethanie just upended when she told me

Cole doesn't know how to play poker. But I'm certain about him being after Bethanie's bank account.

"I'm interested as long as it doesn't involve me. Maybe I can help."

MJ has a point. It always helps when I can talk through clues with someone else, especially if that someone else is a reformed criminal. She'll have insight from the other side, and if I keep the information generic, she doesn't need to know that she probably *is* involved if she knows something about the bodega robbery. But right now, that's the least important aspect of the Cole mystery.

"A friend at school is involved with this guy I think is bad news."

"I know all about that kind of guy. Seems like the only kind I attract," MJ says, and she ain't ever lied. Associating with her last boyfriend is what got her two years in juvie.

"The girl is crazy rich and this guy is really pressing her hard, all charming and everything, and she thinks he's in love with her."

"But he's really after the cheddar."

"I can't make her see it, though. She keeps giving him opportunities to take their romance to the next level, and he won't even kiss her."

"That's weird. Maybe he isn't into girls."

"No, it's definitely not that."

Cole is a mystery, but that I know for sure. No guy could charm a girl—even just look at a girl—the way he can and not be straight. If I wasn't mad about Marco and Cole didn't give me a bad feeling, I'd probably be trying to get him alone for a weekend myself. Not that I'd know what to do with him, but you know what I mean.

"Seems like he'd take her money and whatever else she's throwing at him. That's just how guys are."

"That's what I thought. I just talked to her before you

called and I think he's after a different part of her body—her brain."

"What?"

"This girl is a math genius. She says all the time they're together, he's taking her to the racetrack, having her teach him to count cards and play poker using statistics and probability, encouraging her math skills. That's all they ever do. No movies or putt-putt golf or concerts. None of the usual date stuff."

"If this chick is rich and math smart, he sounds like a gambler who has hit the lottery," MJ says, not knowing how right she is about that lottery part.

"But she had to teach him to play poker. What hard-core gambler doesn't know poker?"

"Maybe he's taking a page from the girl handbook of dating."

There's a handbook? Somebody should have told me because I could seriously use it right about now. "How do you mean?"

"You know, act like you're stupid about something to make a guy feel brilliant. Personally, I think that's some bull—"

"So you're saying he knows how to play," I say, interrupting MJ, back to thinking I did see what I thought I saw last night. "But he's pretending not to know so she can teach him to play better."

"She can teach him to play better *and* he can use her to fund his habit."

"Thanks, MJ, you helped a lot, but I gotta go now," I say, glad she helped me brainstorm. But now I'm ready to think through some things on my own.

"About the bodega thing—"

"I swear, MJ, don't worry. That's the last thing on my mind right now. Talk to you later."

What I told MJ was partly true. I'm not concerned with

her involvement in the holdup—for now—but I'm more certain than ever that Cole somehow staged the whole thing. Now I'm thinking he isn't just a guy with a girl who is so crazy about him she can't see that he's not at all crazy about her, at least not the way she wants him to be.

All those blue ribbons on Bethanie's corkboard in her room—I bet they were for her math skills. They have math bowls that are like spelling bees. They don't get as much press as spelling bees, but if you're good enough to win as many times as Bethanie has, you've probably made the news once or twice. Maybe Cole learned about Bethanie when they were both here in Atlanta—about her math skills and her father's winning lottery ticket—and he tracked her down in Colorado to turn her into his ATM and math coach. What if Cole really is the guy Lana is looking for?

But if Bethanie already has the money and is clearly willing to share her wealth with him, why would he need to gamble at all? I like MJ's theory about the scam he's running on Bethanie, pretending to know nothing about the game so she can teach him, because what girl can pass up the chance to turn a guy into a project? Cole is new to Denver and from what I can guess, he arrived about the same time as the Larsens. Add all that to the fact he has no job but lives large without taking Bethanie's money (so far, anyway), and won't give his last name, and you can see how I'd jump to conclusions.

Lana would probably say my theory is a stretch—too much speculation and not enough evidence. But until I can get another look at the photo in her file, a theory is all I've got.

Chapter 15

When Lana gets back from the Atlanta PD, I realize I've spent an entire day on the Net and turned up nothing. I feel like a bum not only because my research time meant I didn't hang out with my grandparents as much as I should have, I also wasn't able to tell Lana how I single-handedly solved her big case. I was planning to produce proof of my theory that Bethanie was a local math genius in Atlanta on the run from something I haven't figured out yet, but who was followed to Denver by Lana's missing witness because he wanted to use her math skills to win lots of money gambling, like Tom Cruise's character in *Rain Man*. Seriously, that is what I was planning to tell her until this very moment when I realize it sounds insane without proof. I already checked our room. No sign of her case files anywhere. I guess after my snooping last night, she's on to me.

Since I couldn't find any proof on the Net, I need to go right to the source. I find Lana downstairs in the kitchen with my grandmother, helping her clean chitlins at the kitchen sink. The stench hit me before I even got to the kitchen, and yet they're laughing and having a good old time standing over a sink full of pig innards. Yuck!

"You want to help us clean these?" my grandmother asks

like she's offering me tickets to a sold-out Jay-Z concert. "We can make room for you."

"Uh, no, I'm fine over here."

"What Southern girl doesn't like chitlins?"

"I was raised in Colorado. People there don't even know what that is. For good reason."

"But you were born here," my grandmother reminds me, "and you still got South in your blood. You don't know what you're missing."

Yeah, I'm pretty sure I do. But I play nice because I need some information from Lana.

"So how did work go today? Any closer to catching that guy?"

"No closer."

"Any new leads?"

"Nothing new."

Okay, this is getting me nowhere. Lana usually likes to talk a little about her cases, and she wasn't holding out on me last night, but now she's all super quiet. Probably because Grandma's around. She never liked Lana being a cop, thought it was too dangerous for a single mother. She'd really hate it if she knew how much Lana shares her job with me or knew how I secretly want to be a cop—if I can just get over my serious dislike of confrontation and my wussiness in general. I leave them to their mother-daughter bonding over pig intestines and go find my grandfather in the backyard splitting wood.

"Baby girl, you finally come out of your room to visit with me?"

"Sorry I've been AWOL. Trying to keep up with schoolwork since I missed a few days."

"Reminds me of your mama. She stayed in that room all the time, too, when she got to be about your age."

I can't imagine that since when she was my age, she was about to get pregnant with me. Clearly she was leaving her room occasionally.

"You're like her in more ways than one."

"Really? I never thought that at all."

Especially since Lana is fearless, always in control, about four inches taller, and probably never worried about losing ten pounds. And when she was about to turn sixteen, she had a boyfriend with whom she went way past one serious kiss. I present myself as exhibit A.

"Oh, sure. When you were both little girls, you had this curiosity about the world and the way people move through it. It makes your grandmother a little mad, but I wasn't a bit surprised when Lana called us to say she was enrolling in police academy. She tells me you got a little case of the detective bug in you, too. Says it worries her because you're so good at it she can't keep you out of trouble."

"She said I was a good detective?"

"Don't tell her I said so," he says, adding a laugh.

"How else are we alike?" I say, so glad I came to see him.

"Stand away, back there. Don't want any flying wood chips to get you," Papa warns before he raises the ax and brings it down hard against a big piece of white oak. "One thing you definitely have in common is you're both so independent. Act like you don't need anybody or anything."

"That means we know how to take care of ourselves."

"It also means one day when you need some help, and we all do eventually, you won't know how to ask for it."

"We ask for help all the time."

"Only when it comes to helping someone else, never yourself. That doesn't count. Strength is acknowledging where you are weak."

As I watch Papa swing the ax, I don't imagine he has any weaknesses. That's probably because he's the youngest grandfather I know. He's not much older than Tasha's father. I wonder what he thought when Lana first told him about me, and whether she asked him for help then.

As though we conjured her up, Lana comes out to the yard.

"We'll have a nice fire tonight," Papa says.

"Weather this warm would be reason to break out the shorts in Denver, right, Chanti?" Lana says. She sounds happy. I don't know if it's because she's back home or because of the big case, but she's in the perfect mood for me to get some information out of her.

"I know you probably didn't want to talk about the case in front of Grandma, but—"

"Not this time, Chanti, not after the morning I just spent learning about it. The less you know about this case, the better."

"Why's that?"

"See what I mean about you two being so alike?" my grandfather says to me. "Leave her be, Chanti. This is big-time—US Marshals and all that. She can't talk about it."

He splits another log before he stands up straight, stretches his back, and then asks Lana, "Did you make any calls today?"

"At work?"

"No, I mean on personal business."

A look passes between them that tells me they're keeping secrets.

"I was busy."

"He'll just keep on calling here until you do something about it."

"Let him."

"At least give him your number so he'll leave us alone."

"I think he already has it," I say, making them both look at me like they were just remembering I was standing there.

"Who?" Lana turns her eyes on me like I imagine she stares down her perps in the interrogation room.

"I don't know *who*, but I'm guessing y'all are talking about whoever keeps calling home from an Atlanta area code but you keep avoiding. I thought maybe it was an angry perp you arrested, but now I'm thinking it's whoever Papa is talking about. An old boyfriend, maybe?"

I start cheesing like I just solved a big case, but Lana is not at all amused.

"What boyfriend?" Lana asks, sounding angry.

"The one from college you told me about. You know, the one you wanted to marry until you found out he was allergic to children."

"Okay, Chanti, you busted me."

Of course I did. Who else but an ex-boyfriend could be so persistent if it isn't someone she owes money?

"I guess I *am* a good detective," I say, giving Papa a wink. But Lana doesn't appreciate my talents or me sharing insider knowledge with Papa.

"Daddy, I'd appreciate it if you don't bring up this subject again. And you," she says, giving me the evil eye as she starts walking toward the house, "stop minding grown folks' business."

I've seen Lana stop a grown-man fight in the parking lot of Applebee's. She practically had my manager at Tastee Treets crying for his mother when I told Lana he was hitting on me and some of the other girls and she went up there and cursed him out in front of a store full of customers. But whoever the mystery man is that she and my grandparents keep not talking about has her all worked up. Some dude that she hasn't spoken to since college has my take-no-prisoners mother running for cover. Guess I won't be getting that information about her case, after all.

When Lana left for work the next morning she wasn't angry with me anymore, even going out of her way to act especially sweet to me, which tells me that she really doesn't want to share the dirt about her college boyfriend suddenly resurfacing. It seems everyone has a secret but me. I mean a secret about themselves—my secret investigations of Cole and the Larsens don't count. But Lana and her old flame are not on my radar at the moment. I need to check in with Bethanie to see if I can get anything else out of her.

"Did my mom call you yet?" is the first thing Bethanie asks when she answers the phone.

"Yeah, about an hour ago. I felt really bad lying to her."

"Don't even try it, Chanti. I've heard you tell a lie or two."

"Not like this. Little lies don't hurt, and I try to do it only when telling the truth will hurt someone's feelings, but nothing else."

"Or when you're playing Nancy Drew."

"That's not hurting anyone—that's *helping*."

"Depends on who you ask."

"Such attitude you have this morning. Don't forget I'm helping you," I remind her.

"I know. I'm sorry. It's just that it isn't going the way I hoped."

"Strip poker didn't work out?"

"No, and neither has anything else I've tried. He seems more like my babysitter than my boyfriend," she says, and I can hear her disappointment.

"Bethanie, has he actually called himself your boyfriend?"

"No, but he doesn't need to. He's always wanting to be with me, and this weekend was his idea, not mine. You said yourself he stalked me just to meet me at the bodega."

"True," I say, before adding in what I hope sounds like a joking tone, "Maybe he just wants you for your money. You're his sugar mama."

"A week ago that comment would have pissed me off, but now I'm starting to wonder."

"Oh yeah?"

"Except that I haven't spent a dime on him. Not that I haven't tried. He won't let me. We split the tab on everything.

And now my father has my money on lock, so I couldn't spend anything on him if I wanted to."

I remember Mr. Larsen saying he was going to decrease her allowance. I guess he made good on that. Which sucks because my entire theory about Cole being after her for her money is shot, unless he's setting the stage that he's just a nice guy and later starts mooching off her. I latch on to the weaker part of my theory.

"If he's not after your money, maybe he wants you to teach him how to win at poker. Does he have a gambling problem?"

"Why would you even say that? What are you trying to insinuate?" Bethanie's entire tone changes and she's back to being all sensitive and paranoid.

"Well, he joked about it at dinner the night we double dated, and you said he kept taking you to the dog track. I was just throwing out ideas of why he wants to hang with you so much but hasn't made a single move, that's all."

"It was a joke, and he never places a bet, remember? Some of the stuff you come up with is just so out there, Chanti. I have to go. I probably won't talk to you anymore until I see you in school."

"Wait a minute, Bethanie. . . ." I say, but all I get is a dead line.

So Cole isn't after her money—at least not yet—but that doesn't mean the rest of my theory is wrong. He really could be a gambler looking to improve his odds with Bethanie's help. Maybe he *is* the guy Lana is looking for, a desperate guy on the run who just happened to find a Bonnie to play against his Clyde, a crazy rich Bonnie, no less.

Chapter 16

Lana and I are on our way to do some shopping when she gets a call. I pick up her cell because Lana won't talk on the phone while she's driving, but I know for a fact that's only when I'm in the car. I guess she's trying to set a good example or something, since she's already terrified of me turning sixteen soon and getting behind the wheel.

"Lana Evans's phone."

"This is Detective Sanders," says the familiar voice. "Is Evans available?"

"She's driving at the moment. Whenever I'm in the car, she pretends she doesn't use her phone while driving."

Detective Sanders laughs before saying, "You must be Chanti."

"All day long. Can I take a message for her?"

"Can she swing by the department? We have some new information that we'd like her input on, and I know y'all are heading back to Colorado tomorrow."

"You mean right now? On a Saturday?"

"If that wouldn't be a problem," the detective replies in a tone that says *it better not be a problem.*

By now Lana is making faces at me trying to get information on who's calling, and becoming more distracted from the road than if she had just taken the call herself.

"Not at all," I say, making an executive decision and ignoring Lana's gesticulations. "We're on Interstate Eighty-five now, just a few miles from downtown, so we should be there in less than ten minutes."

"Who was that?"

"Detective Sanders. They have some new developments on the case and want you to come right over. I knew you'd want to, so I answered for you."

"I wonder what's going on," she says excitedly, and then remembers the day we had planned. "Do you mind, Chanti? Maybe this won't take too long. I could take you back home and pick you up later."

"That's why you're here, remember? I don't mind at all. And there's no time to take me home—I told her we'd be there in a few minutes. She sounded really impatient, like she had to talk to you right now."

It couldn't have worked out more perfectly if I had planned it. Now maybe I'll get a little information on this case, and see if I'm even close on my speculations about Cole being the runaway witness.

When we arrive at Atlanta PD, Detective Sanders meets us at the employee entrance and leads the way to the detective bureau. The police department seems about like any other, except more quiet since it's Saturday; mostly uniforms work on Saturday and they're all out patrolling. If something goes down on the street that requires a detective, like a homicide or a big drug bust, a patrol officer will contact an on-call detective. At least that's how it works in Lana's department. I guess some detectives are working this weekend because when we get to Sanders's desk, there are several of them there. This must be a big case if this many detectives are in on a Saturday morning.

"Can I get you a soda or something, Chanti?" Sanders offers.

"No, thank you, ma'am. I'm fine. I'll just sit here listening to music and catching up on my e-mail," I say, holding up my phone as proof. I put my ear buds in and pretend to be instantly engrossed in texting. I want them to forget I'm even in the room. They totally buy my act, which I knew they would since, according to Lana and every other parent I know, they think we'll all develop carpal tunnel from texting, go deaf from playing our music so loudly, and grow a brain tumor from holding the phone to our heads all day long.

Sanders walks up to a big map on the wall, which I know right away is the map they're using to track the runaway witness's movements. If you watch a lot of TV like I do, you'd think the cops would use some kind of wall-sized GPS system and just wave their hands in front of it to change the location or terrain or something, but really they use a big old map with pushpins just like they did back in the day. Not only do I not look up directly at the map, I even dance around in my seat a little like I'm getting into my music when really the volume is off. Once they all turn to watch Sanders, then I get a good look at it.

"I've changed my theory on the case since yesterday and want to run it by all of you. We already know through our casino surveillance that the subject has been moving west, hitting casinos in Mississippi, Missouri, Kansas," Sanders says. "Originally, we were only tracking his movement by watching points of egress at the casinos. Then we started watching his actual gambling activity and noticed that as he makes his way west, he's been increasing his stakes."

"How much?" asks Lana.

"First he seemed to be gambling only for entertainment—very small stakes. By the time he reached Kansas, he was hitting the high table limits."

"Where's he getting the money?" asks a very cute detective.

"Exactly," Sanders says. "He owes money to several dangerous people so we know for a fact he didn't have any, certainly not the amounts he's been throwing around at blackjack tables. If he had it, he would have paid them off rather than come to us with a deal."

"He may have stashed something away, with plans to run. Probably what he stole from the Boss," Lana offers.

The Boss. I make a mental note of that even if it isn't a real name. It must be a code word for the guy the missing witness was supposed to testify against. I could take notes on my phone, or record the whole conversation, but it isn't worth getting caught when I'll just remember everything anyway.

"I doubt he had that much stashed away, not unless he robbed the Federal Reserve or won the sweepstakes," says the detective. Okay, he's cute, but he didn't have to check Lana like that.

"He stayed on the move, presumably to keep us from finding him. After a few weeks at the tables in Kansas, he dropped off radar. First we assumed he continued moving west through Colorado without gambling because stakes were really low in that state."

"But . . . ?"

"Colorado recently raised their limits—not Vegas stakes but high enough to bring him back into the casinos," Sanders explains. "An addict won't stay away too long, no matter how risky it is for him to surface."

"That's why you called Denver in," Lana says. "You know he's there."

"Unfortunately we aren't sure. Our last tape of him is over a month old. He resurfaced shortly after the stakes were raised, but only for a week or so, then we lost him again. I thought maybe he had run out of money or got bored with limited stakes and moved on to Nevada, which his pattern so far indicated he would do. But I figured if he had been in Denver recently, your department could at least pick up his trail faster than we could, even if he'd already left town."

"Now you have a new theory."

"He hasn't shown up in Nevada yet, or anywhere outside Colorado. It could mean he kicked the habit, but I doubt it. I think something spooked him, scared him enough to finally stay under, and we know it wasn't us because he's always been ahead of us. We didn't think to watch the casinos until he'd been on the run awhile, so everything we're looking at is old news."

"Right. You told us yesterday the Marshals Service was on him," says a detective sitting next to Lana.

"That's what I thought at first. They haven't been especially forthright with us with that whole *need to know basis* bull—"

She stops talking and though I never look up, I can hear them all turn in their seats to look in my direction, presumably because Sanders almost used a *bad word* in front of me. Yeah, keep right on thinking I'm just a kid, and keep right on talking while you're at it. My thumbs pound away at my phone's keyboard and I dance around in my chair a little for added effect. They resume the conversation.

"It could be the marshals, but now I'm thinking it might be the Boss."

"But how?" asks Detective Cute.

"If *we* know his penchant for gambling, you know the Boss does. That's the whole reason he's after him."

"If the Boss has him, our case is done."

"That's where Evans and her department come in. The Boss might have him, but the other possibility is the witness figured out the Boss was on his tail and went into hiding. People always think it's easier to hide in a small town, but you can really disappear in a larger city and those are hard to come by out west until you reach California. I think he's still hiding out in Denver somewhere."

"He could have gone south to Dallas or Houston. Maybe Phoenix," Lana offers.

"I don't think so. I think he was hell-bent on getting to Las Vegas. I've watched hours of tape on him. I spent a lot of time with the guy, during interrogation and at the safe house, and he was always talking about those poker tournaments on ESPN and how he was going to Vegas so he could beat Doyle Brunson."

"Who's that?" Lana asks.

"I don't know, some god among poker players, I guess. There isn't much casino action between Denver and Las Vegas, so I figure he's lying low there, blending in until he gets up either the nerve, the money, or both to move on to Vegas. He may have gotten a job if he's run out of money."

"A nine-to-five?" says the hottie. "That guy hasn't lived a straight day in his life."

"Which is why I think he knows the Boss is after him. He literally has been scared straight by something."

"I'll put in a call to my department now," Lana says. "I'll give them all the details tomorrow, but at least we can get a BOLO out on him."

Lana walks away from the group to find a phone, pretty much out of my hearing range, which sucks because I know if she's going to establish a Be On the Lookout Order, she'll be giving someone a description. Atlanta PD will send Denver an official description, too, but I know for a fact she's calling her partner first. I only pick up on a few snippets, but not enough to make sense of anything. The one solid piece of information I do get is nothing I want to hear. The missing witness is a forty-seven-year-old male, which means he isn't Cole. I guess a picture can sometimes lie.

Chapter 17

With new information that the perp might be in the Denver area, Lana cut our trip a day short and got us on the last flight out. We didn't get in from the airport until after midnight, so I'm in deep sleep when my phone rings the next morning and I have to run around the house trying to figure out where I left it. I find my bag in the living room and dig out the phone on the last ring, hopefully before Lana heard it. When I see Bethanie's number on caller ID, I'm ticked. Not only was I asleep, but she didn't call me when she was supposed to, didn't answer her phone when I tried to call her, and has me more than a little worried.

"Where've you been?" I ask without a hello.

"Excuse me?" It's not the voice I expected.

"I'm sorry, Mrs. Larsen. I didn't check caller ID and thought you'd be a friend calling."

"I know your mama taught you better than to answer a phone like that."

"Yes, ma'am."

"Now then, I need to speak to Bethanie."

"Right now?"

"That would be why I called *right now*. She said she was gonna let me know whether she's staying over there another night. If she is, Mr. Larsen and I were thinking of spending another night in Black Hawk."

If Bethanie is going to use me as her alibi, she could at least let me in on the story I'm supposed to be telling.

"Um, yes, Mrs. Larsen, I do believe she's planning to stay over another night."

"Do you mind if I just ask her myself?"

"Of course not, but she's in the shower right now."

"Y'all must have one nice shower over there—the girl lives in that shower."

I forgot that was the excuse I used last time she called. "Yes, ma'am. I'll have her call you when she's out."

It's bad enough I have to lie to Mrs. Larsen, but at least I can handle her. Now I hear Lana in the kitchen, and lying to her is a whole other thing. Have you ever tried lying to the person who knows you best in the world when she makes a living catching people in their lies? I'm very good at it, but that doesn't mean it's an easy thing to do. When I walk into the kitchen, she's got one hand on her hip, using the other to lean against the counter. She looks like she was very much asleep until three minutes ago. I don't like my mother when she's sleep deprived. No one does.

"Who the hell is calling here at eight o'clock on a Sunday morning?" She grabs my phone from my hand and holds it up in my face for emphasis, or evidence, I'm not sure.

"Eight is not *that* early."

"I pay the bills around here, and if I say eight is early, it's early." Lana is always surly when you wake her before she planned on waking, but it's okay because she's also a little slow on the draw and a lot easier to fool.

"It was Marco wanting to talk," I say, wishing that was true.

"I thought he was . . ." Lana says, trying to find a delicate way to say *out of the picture,* which is tough when she's still half asleep and not in a delicate mood at all.

"We're trying to work things out."

"Well, I'm glad ya'll made up, but can't he call you at a decent hour?"

"I'll tell him not to call before ten from now on."

"All right," she says, planting a kiss on my forehead, which I don't remember her doing in forever. "If you need to talk later, we can."

"Thanks, Mom."

"I'm going back to bed. Put this on vibrate," she says, handing me my phone.

Once I know Lana is in bed and probably asleep, I throw on some clothes and leave the house as quietly as possible. No sense in waking her again when I call Bethanie to curse her out, so I'll do a walk-and-talk up the block. If I wasn't awake before, the cold morning has slapped any leftover sleep right out of me. I should have worn a hat and scarf because my ears are freezing. Another reason to curse Bethanie.

"I am so through with you," I say when Bethanie answers.

"Did my mom call?"

"Of course she called, asking to talk to you, and I had no idea what you told her about how long you'd be staying with me."

"I know, I know. I forgot to tell you the whole plan."

"Why didn't you answer last night?"

"You're worse than my father. You don't have to check up on me, Chanti. Cole is not some criminal. I thought you trusted him by now."

"I do," I lie. Even if he isn't the missing informant, he's still shady. "But I'm starting to feel weird lying to your parents, especially when I keep having to tell your mom you're in the shower."

"Don't be mad at me, Chanti. I'm so, so happy today. I want you to be happy for me."

"Why so happy today? Did he finally come around to . . . you know?"

"This is love. I'm in love. I promise, this is the last time you have to cover for me. Monday at school I'll be able to tell you everything, and tell my parents everything."

"Everything about what?"

"It's a surprise for now."

"Okay, but you'd better tell me *everything*. And be at school early because I won't be able to wait until lunch."

"That's the least I owe you."

"Damn skippy," I say, feeling apprehensive about whatever Bethanie's mystery is but also glad I'll be seeing her tomorrow and this whole stupid charade will be over. "Where *are* you anyway? What's all that noise this early in the morning? Sounds like you're at an amusement park."

"Something like that," she says again. "I have to go now."

"What about your mom? She wants to know if you're sleeping over again because she wants to stay another night in Black Hawk."

"Black Hawk? So my dad's trying to go it alone."

"He isn't alone. He's with your mother."

"Never mind. I'll call my mom after I hang up with you."

"What if she asks why you're calling from your cell instead of from my house?"

"Uh, you're confusing my mother with yours. Mine will never even notice that."

"So can you at least give me a hint about your surprise?"

"Seriously, Chanti, I have to go. I promise, Monday."

And then she's gone.

A few hours have passed since I spoke to her and I still don't feel right about Bethanie's surprise. It could be that she and Cole finally got busy, which would explain all the *I'm in love* talk. I don't know about it personally, but I remember when Michelle gave it up to her sorry ex-boyfriend Donnell, everything out of her mouth about him was love this and love that. I know Bethanie has been on a mission to defy her parents, but I'm pretty sure that isn't something she'd be excited to share with them unless she's even weirder than I thought.

Since I do my best thinking over something good to eat, I'm sitting in my favorite booth at Tastee Treets when I see Marco walk in with some girl. I immediately ascertain she's a skank, though anyone else without my keen sense of observation might think she's a nice girl since on the brief walk between the door and the counter, she manages to hold the door open for an old man, give napkins to a little kid who can't reach them, and help clean up the same kid's spilled soda. She's totally overcompensating for knowing that in truth, she's a skank.

Marco doesn't notice me, but I have a clear view of them at the counter. I can't hear what they're saying but I can tell from his gestures that they have a history, and not a he's-just-a-friend history. They're standing too close together, everything she says is funny to him, and in a very simple transaction of burger ordering, they each find about three reasons to touch one another—on the shoulders, back, arm— everywhere considered decent to touch in public. I'm pretty sure Marco and this girl never had the problems Bethanie was having with Cole. She must be Angelique, Marco's ex. Well, not his ex because clearly that status now belongs to me.

When they turn from the counter in search of a table, Marco sees me. At first he looks completely shocked and slightly embarrassed, but quickly regains his usual take-everything-in-stride attitude and whispers something to Angelique, who looks at me and smiles. Someone else might think it was the kind of smile you give to someone you genuinely feel sorry for, like a friend who just told you she didn't make the drama club when all she's dreamt about since birth was acting. I see it for the evil smirk that it really is. Marco hands her the tray, which she carries to a table on the other side of the restaurant, and he walks toward me.

"Hey, Chanti. I didn't expect to see you here."

"Yeah, I only live a block away, used to work here, and told you a couple of times that I'm pretty much always here."

I surprise myself by how much I sound like a jilted girl on an MTV reality show. I know girls who do that whole swiveling-head, finger-in-his-face boyfriend drama thing, but I never knew I was one of them.

"Well, I live twelve blocks from here and they have the absolute best chocolate shakes. A friend told me about them," he says, then smiles like he's really here on a date with me, not that . . . girl.

"I thought I was more than a friend."

"Like I thought I was more important than your crazy obsession with playing detective. Not just crazy, but dangerous."

"But that's what I do. It's part of who Chanti is. Why can't you accept me the way I am?"

Did I just say that? Seriously, *I'm* not quite sure who I am at this very moment, because I've gone from an MTV reality show chick to a Hollywood movie queen who refers to herself in the third person.

"I'd never try to change you because a lot of that is why I think you're so great. It's just that maybe you aren't great for me."

"But I guess we can still be friends, right?" I say this in a tone that clearly implies we will not be friends.

"There's the whole thing with my parents. They have a legit concern that hanging with you is a little dangerous, but you just keep right on doing stuff that will probably get you in trouble, even though you know it'll make it tough for us to be together."

"One time. It only happened one time."

"Well, when you're just a few seconds from being killed,

one time is enough. Besides, we both know that won't be the only time. Before I walked up, you were probably trying to figure out if Bethanie's boyfriend is a bad guy, right?"

No, I was thinking how if I had any kind of nerve I'd go up to you and that . . . girl and go swivel-headed drama chick on y'all. Before *that* I was trying to figure out if Bethanie's boyfriend is a bad guy. See how much you know? Of course, I don't say any of this because the passive-aggressive Chanti I know and love is back (except for the referring to myself in third person part) and now all I can do is pout and say nothing.

"Chanti, I need a girl who really wants to be with me, not just when she can fit me in between cases, especially when she's not actually a cop and there isn't actually a case."

"You mean a girl like Angelique."

"I should get back to her now," he says, looking at me in a way that confuses me because I can swear his eyes are saying something different—that he'd rather stay here with me.

"Yeah, you should," I say, because as long as he walked in here with some other girl, there's really no reason for me to be confused.

"But we'll still see each other at school, right?"

"Oh, would that be the school Angelique said she wanted you to drop out of because going there instead of North High was like saying you thought you were better than she was? Wasn't that the reason y'all broke up?"

"She sees things differently now. She doesn't want to change me anymore."

"Ironic."

"Like I said, Chanti, I don't want to change you. It's just we aren't right for each other."

"Whatever. Go."

As he walks away, I noisily draw the last of my melted shake through the straw for reasons unknown to me except I really have no idea how to break up with a boyfriend, though

I'm sure slurping isn't the lasting impression you want your ex to have of you. I'm grateful to be sitting near the back door so I won't have to see Angelique and her evil smirk/pity smile when I leave. And I'm sad not only because I've been officially dumped but also because the Tastee Treets is now off-limits. I really do love these shakes, especially at a time like this.

Chapter 18

It's Monday morning and not only does Bethanie not show up early, she isn't at school by first bell. When she hasn't found me by second period or even sent a text to tell me what's up, I'm beyond mad. And when no one has seen her by lunch, I'm beyond worried. The only good thing about worrying over Bethanie is that it keeps me from being sick over losing Marco. I managed to not see him the first half of the day. And because I'm so stressed wondering if she's dead or alive, I can't even focus on school, so I'm going off campus during lunch to find Miss Bethanie. She'd better be alive because I plan to set her straight about standing me up. If I'm lucky, I'll avoid Marco after lunch, too, since we don't have any Monday classes in the same hall. I know I'll have to deal with seeing him eventually since we both have another year and a half at Langdon, but I can only handle one crisis at a time.

The address Bethanie gave me for Cole's place is just a few miles from school and I figure if I can get down the hill and reach the crosstown bus in time, I should be able to get there, curse out Bethanie, and if she's still willing to give me a ride back to school after I tell her exactly what I think about her and her boyfriend, I might only miss the first half of fifth period. While I run to make the bus, I dial Bethanie's number one more time to see if I was wrong about the new development that has me so worried. No, I hear the same message for the third time: *this number is no longer in service.*

By the time I get off the bus in front of Cole's building, I've had enough time to go from mad worried, to just plain mad, to making deals with God that if Bethanie is okay, I promise not to curse her out, at least not until tomorrow. I'm relieved to find it's actually an apartment building, though it looks a little run-down for GQ Cole. Even though Bethanie said he's just here temporarily, it's hard to imagine Cole staying one night. At least it's a real place. The whole bus ride over, I kept imagining the address was a fake and would lead me to a 7-Eleven. Bethanie would probably expect me to check it out online to make sure she wasn't scamming me, which makes me wonder now why I hadn't. Thinking about Marco definitely has me off my game, but now he's Angelique's worry, not mine. As soon as she reminds him why he dropped her in the first place, she'll be the one up late at night crying and wishing she had a chocolate shake to drown her sorrow.

When I get off the elevator and make my way to Cole's place, I find the door open to an empty apartment, except for a cleaning crew. I check my notes again, glad I didn't rely on memory this time because I must have written down the wrong apartment number. No, it matches the one on the door. So that means I must have the wrong street address, or the wrong street. I definitely got something very, very wrong.

Just then a woman comes out of what must be the bed-room.

"Make sure you clean the refrigerator," she tells the cleaning crew. "Take whatever you want. He must have just gone shopping, because it's full. Who are you?"

"I'm looking for a friend, but I must have the wrong apartment."

"Was it the guy who just moved out? Because if it is, maybe you can tell me how to find him. He didn't tell me where to send his deposit."

"Was his name Cole?" I ask, hoping it wasn't, because if it was it would mean I have absolutely no idea where Bethanie is.

"That's it."

"Did he live alone?"

"Thought you said you were a friend."

"I'm really looking for someone else, a girl. Cole was, is her boyfriend."

"Oh yeah. There was a girl here when he asked me to come by and get the rent."

"How'd she look?"

"What do you mean, how'd she look? She was pretty, about your age. I thought maybe a bit too young for him, but what do I know. In my day, college boys wouldn't be caught with a high school girl, and of course, all we wanted to catch was a college boy," she says, laughing like we have a private joke. She's getting lost in memories of ancient times when I'm just trying to find out where Bethanie and Cole are.

"I mean, did she look sad or worried or something?"

"Look, I don't want trouble around here 'cause I run a nice building. Were they into something bad?"

"No, nothing like that. It's just they were having a few problems. She was thinking about breaking up with him."

"Didn't look that way to me. She looked as happy as I'd have been when I was her age and landed a nice-looking college boy like that, and one with some money, too."

"Do you know where he went to college?"

"Seems like your *friend* didn't tell you too much about him, did she? I just assumed from his age that he was a college boy, but now that I think about it, I don't think I ever saw him go to school."

"Do you know where he worked?"

"He didn't, unless he worked the graveyard shift. Nearly every night, he left around ten o'clock, didn't come back until dawn. I figured he had a girl somewhere. Not that I was watching him," she says, then points to the floor. "I'm in the apartment below, and I'm a light sleeper."

"What makes you think he had money? If he had money, he'd probably stay somewhere else. No offense."

"Some taken. I rent month to month. The fact he didn't have a job but paid me three months rent ahead of time, plus a month deposit, all in cash, was a clue. Most folks barely want to pay me for one month."

She must have a higher regard for her building than I do.

"Four months of whatever you charge for rent at this place, even in cash, doesn't make a guy rich," I say. "Sounds more like a guy who doesn't want to be found."

"Maybe, but you can always tell a man with money, even one who's just barely a man. You probably don't know that since you're just a girl yet."

"School me, then."

"Maybe you ain't such a girl after all," she says, giving me a once-over. "Sound more like a cop."

"In this school uniform?"

This seems to allay her concern that she might be talking to a fifteen-year-old police officer.

"He drove a real nice car."

"That was her car, not his."

"Were you here? No, I didn't think so."

She walks to a window and gestures for me to follow.

"That there is her car."

She points at what looks to be Bethanie's car in the parking lot below. I feel sick, but manage to suppress the nausea that always comes when I'm really scared.

"He drove one of those expensive sporty cars. You remember that boy's car, Roland?"

"Yeah, it was a Porsche—silver 911 GT3 with a rear

spoiler," says the guy who'd been pushing a carpet cleaner when I first arrived.

"Roland's got a keen eye. Just wish he'd use it on the job. You missed a spot there."

I look down at the carpet and the missed spot.

"Does that look like blood to you?" I ask.

"Could be, now you mention it," Roland says.

"Like I said, looked to me like those kids were in love, and you're making trouble where there is none, little girl. I don't let bad elements lease my place."

"I'm sure it's nothing," I say, not believing myself for a second.

"I think they had even been on a picnic, which isn't something a fighting couple would do."

"Why do you think that?"

"Not that I'm nosy or anything, just wanted to get a good look at his fancy car. Saw he had picnic-type things in the backseat—a little cooler, a blanket."

Well, that doesn't give me much to work with.

"Can I take a look around the apartment?"

"Sure, but there's nothing to see."

She's right. I walk through all the rooms and find nothing to tell me anything about Bethanie's stay here or where they might be now.

The rental agent, still standing by the window when I return to the living room, asks, "About that deposit—do you know where I can find him?"

"I wish I did. When did he leave?"

"Saturday morning. Told me I could keep the third month's rent even though he was here less than two. Didn't say anything about what to do with the deposit. Must have been in a hurry because he left a refrigerator full of food."

"He must not have been in too much of a hurry," I add. "He had time to pack everything."

Since my most recent employment was in the moving

business, I know exactly what it takes to move an apartment this size. He must have planned to leave at least a day out, or maybe from the moment he out-of-the blue asked Bethanie to stay with him for the weekend.

"You really must not be that close a friend," she says, looking skeptical again. "He didn't have much of anything to pack. He rented a bed, table, two chairs. I had to call the rental company to have it moved out. But he left some money for my trouble. Says it all right here in this note."

"Can I see it?"

"Nothing in it but instructions to call the rental company," she says, handing me the note.

She's right. There's nothing here that might give me a clue what the hell is up with Cole. At the end of the note, he apologizes for inconveniencing the leasing agent. A serial killer wouldn't do that, would he? I hand the note back to her.

"Keep it," she says. "What I need is his forwarding address."

"So do I."

"Well, if I can't find him, I guess I can't give him his deposit, right? When you hear from him, tell him not to accuse me of keeping his money."

Of course I don't go back to school, but go home to think through everything and wait out the rest of the school day until I can go to Bethanie's house. I'm still hoping that she's somehow lost phone coverage, decided to spend another day with Cole wherever he is, before going home tonight where she'll pick up on her original plan of saying she went to school from my house this morning. I wonder who she got to call Langdon and lie to Smythe. Probably Cole. Everything about him is a big fat lie. I check messages, praying Bethanie has left one of them, but it's only Lana saying she's missing a case file and asking me to check around her desk to see if she left it somewhere.

I find the file in the trash can beside her desk. It must have fallen off the tower of folders, papers, and notebooks. Considering she's in a business where details are everything, and she's very good at it, Lana is kind of messy. Okay, very messy—I barely found the desk. I try to decide if I should call Lana and let her know I found it, which would give it away that I'm home an hour early, or if that even matters, because if Bethanie is somewhere with Cole Whoever-He-Is, me skipping school is the least of my worries. In fact, it's probably time I come clean with Lana because this whole thing is starting to feel way out of my league.

I take a look in the file hoping it's related to her big Atlanta case, but it's something about a carjacking in Denver. While I'm dialing Lana's number at the police department, I notice the corner of a photo stuck in the sliver of space between her desk and filing cabinet. When I rescue the photo from the Bermuda Triangle that is Lana's desk, I find a shot of three men standing on a sidewalk, talking. I'm about to put it on top of a stack of paper when a guy in the background of the photo catches my eye. To the left of the three men and almost clipped out of the picture is a car with its driver's door open, a younger man either getting in or out, I can't really tell. All the photographer got of him is his head above the car door. But that's enough for me because even though he is slightly out of focus, I'm pretty sure the driver is Cole. Maybe that other photo I saw in Atlanta didn't lie to me after all.

I hang up the phone and look through the mess on Lana's desk for other pictures, hoping for some clue of why Cole would be in one of Lana's photos, but there are none, so I study this one a little closer. The car he's getting out of—it's silver. There's an icon on the hood and it's in focus because the other three men in the photo are standing near the front of the car, but it's too small to make it out. I grab my phone and take a picture of the photo so I can blow it up on my laptop.

Score—the car is a silver Porsche, which is what Roland from the apartment cleaning crew said Cole was driving. Even if he wasn't the target of the photographer and was just a bystander, he couldn't be an innocent one. That's just too much coincidence. Maybe I was right about Cole being the missing suspect.

But Lana definitely said he was a middle-aged guy. If Cole was the suspect, the photographer would have him in focus, and those other guys would be in the background. Why would he be anywhere near Lana's investigation, even if he wasn't an actual target? He did say he's from some town outside Atlanta. I suppose he could have just been in the wrong place at the wrong time. I've been there a few times myself. Except Cole is making a serious habit of it—at the bodega, then at Bethanie's car when the thug was waiting for her, now in this photo. According to him, he hasn't been in Atlanta in a long time, but there he is getting out of a car on Peachtree Street in Midtown. I know the restaurant those guys are standing in front of. The back of the photo is dated six weeks ago. I don't know why he'd be in this photo, or why he'd lie about not being in Atlanta recently, but I get the feeling it isn't because he's just some gold digger.

I'm thinking he's a whole lot worse.

Chapter 19

I know I should involve Lana at this point, and I will, but first I need the kind of information on Cole I could get from a more reliable source than I could get from her. Whatever his story is, Lana will only give me the whitewashed version, if she tells me anything at all. No matter how good a police investigation is going, they never know as much about it as the street knows. That's why they spend all that money on confidential informants. I don't have any money, but I do have a friend who is just as good as any CI, and I'm hoping MJ can help me figure out who Cole is and how dangerous he might be. MJ has sworn off the life, but I know she still has plenty of connections. I just have to convince her to use them to help me.

When MJ opens her door, she actually looks relieved to see me.

"Chanti, you're right on time."

"For what?"

"Wait a minute. You're not here to ask me about the bodega, are you?"

"You don't have to worry about me getting in your business. I'm still dealing with my other friend's problem. So why are you glad to see me?"

"You know how I'm trying to get my GED? I got this science exam Friday and I have to pass or they'll make me re-take the class. You're like a genius and whatnot, right?"

"I wouldn't say genius, but science is my thing. What are you studying?"

"Biology, and it's kicking my butt."

"All right, I'll help you with your exam, but you have to help me first, and it's big."

"How big?"

"Remember that friend I was telling you about, the one I thought has a boyfriend who's a gold digger?"

"The rich friend who has you so busy solving her prob-lems that you ain't got time for MJ? Yeah, I remember," she says. I guess I'm not off the hook for acting like she doesn't live down the block from me, and for barely talking to her since the Donnell situation. But I don't have time to fix that now.

"I think dude is more than a gold digger. Like maybe he's in some gang or maybe even a crime family. Do you have any contacts in Atlanta who could tell me something about him?"

"Chanti, you know I'm trying to live straight now—get my GED, not make my grandmother sorry she let me come live here, much less violate my parole. Making a call like that is like making a recovering chocoholic walk through the Hershey factory."

"I know, and I wouldn't ask if it wasn't serious. Here, I wrote down some information I have on him, including a physical description," I say, handing her my notes. "I only have a first name."

"It's probably an alias, but maybe I can get something off the description and his timing in Denver and Atlanta," MJ says, reading over my notes.

"You think your friend is involved with whatever this dude is into?"

"She doesn't have a clue, which is probably safer for her right now."

"Just how rich is she?"

"I'll tell you after you make that call."

"Well, she better be cash reward rich," MJ says. She looks reluctant but leaves me in the living room to go make the call from her bedroom. I guess after learning my mother is a cop, she still doesn't trust me. A couple of minutes later, she returns.

"Where's Big Mama?" I ask.

"Still at work. She'll be home soon, though, so you should probably make it a quick visit. She don't like you much."

"Yeah, that seems to be a theme, but at least we're even on that front. You aren't my mother's favorite person, either."

"I saved your butt and your mother still got beef with me?" she says, but doesn't wait for my answer. " 'S a'ight. I got issues with her, too."

We're quiet for a minute, but I don't want MJ to start thinking about how much she hates cops and how she thinks I betrayed her because I'm pretty sure I'm going to need her help beyond that one phone call, so I tell her everything I know and suspect about Cole. Just as I finish my debriefing, her phone rings and she leaves me alone in the living room again.

"That was quick," I say when she returns, hopeful that such a fast callback meant no one had ever heard of him.

"It was quick because they didn't need to look deep to find someone who knows about this guy Cole, 'cept they call him Coleman. That's his last name."

"So much for that story about last names denoting ownership," I say, recalling the lame excuse he gave during the double date.

"What?"

"Nothing. What else did you find out?"

"Your guess was right. He's part of a crime family down there."

"Like the Mafia?"

"Not the Mafia, but something like it. A small-time version of it but still badass. My contact is still checking for more information, but they do know dude came out of nowhere and all *Donnie Brasco*-style got in good with the head of the Family."

"This is bad."

"Real bad. What made you connect some preppie gold digger to a crime family, anyway? Something you not telling me?"

"It's just the way he carried himself, and I've watched too many mob movies, I guess."

"So have I, but I can't name one with a mobster who looks like he shops at Eddie Bauer, which is how you describe him."

I completely trust MJ. She hasn't busted Lana on being a cop yet when, given how mad she was with me and how she hates the police, she could have told everyone on the block by now. I want her to know that I trust her, because I'm going to need her help, but I don't tell her anything about Lana's case being connected to a crime family or about the photo of Cole. I figure MJ didn't need to know that, and it's probably safer it she didn't. Except maybe not. I just remembered the secret she's keeping about Eddie, mystery bodega man. I'll have to get that information out of her soon, but since her trust in me is fragile to nonexistent, I'll hold off on that for now.

"I'd better go call my mother. This thing is way past what I can do to help Bethanie."

"Much as I hate to call the cops for any reason, I think you're right. I'll let you know if I hear anything else," MJ says, walking me to the door. "Hey, what about my bio homework?"

"Let me tell my mother what you found out and then I'll come back."

"Maybe by then you'll be willing to tell me the rest of the story."

I head back to my house thinking that if I can believe all those mob movies, that photo means Cole must be a driver for someone high up in the Family. But why in the world would he be in Denver if the Family is based in Atlanta, and what would he want from Bethanie? Yeah, he wants her money, but how did he know she had any, and what made him come halfway across the country to find out that she did? I couldn't find a thing during my Internet searches about the Larsens winning the Powerball. I have a lot more questions than answers, but one thing I know for sure. Bethanie isn't just dating Cole. She's disappeared with him.

Chapter 20

Before I can step off MJ's porch, my phone rings. I don't recognize the number so I'm surprised when I hear Bethanie's voice.

"Don't be mad at me, Chanti."

"I probably should be ticked when you keep starting our conversations like that," I say, but I'm soooo not mad at her. I'm just relieved to be hearing from her at all.

"Sorry I ditched you at school today, but I had a great reason to."

"I'm coming over there now so you can tell me all about it."

"Don't. I'm not at home. That's why I'm calling."

"Are you at his—Cole's place? I don't recognize the number you called from," I say, wondering if she'll lie. Wherever she is sounds like one huge party, same as when I spoke to her yesterday morning. Did she ditch me to go to the circus?

"Oh, that. I'm using one of those prepaid phones. Cole suggested we get rid of my phone once I told him you like to play Nancy Drew and if anyone came looking for us, you'd be the one who could tell them how to find us."

Not a single part of her last sentence made any sense.

Bethanie normally acts like her phone has national security secrets imbedded in it, but Cole tells her to get rid of it and she just does it. Who would come looking for them and why don't they want to be found? I try to think up the best way to ask both those questions so I still sound like her supportive friend instead of her extremely freaked out friend who really wants to say WTF about five thousand times and demand she get her butt home now.

"Okay, Bethanie. Who would be trying to track you down?"

"My parents when I don't walk through the front door in about thirty minutes like I always do. They'll come looking for you and as good as you are at lying, you can't fool them forever."

"You're saying all of this like you're telling me about some boring thing that happened in the cafeteria at school. But what it sounds like you're saying is you've run off with Cole and you don't want anyone to find you. I can barely hear what you're saying. Are you still at that amusement park you were at yesterday?"

"The way you say it makes it sound kind of crazy, but it really isn't."

"No, it really is," I say, realizing I'm not faking the supportive friend thing very well. "A guy who tells you to ditch your phone so you can't be tracked is *totally* crazy, not 'kind of' crazy. I don't care how much he wants to be with you in spite of your parents' disapproval, that is just geeked up."

"I don't need all this negativity when I'm so happy. I'm going to hang up if—"

"No wait. It's just a lot to take in, Bethanie. You can see how I might be a little upset, right?"

"Only because you're you and you worry about everything. I'm fine. I'm better than fine, and soon I'll be home and I can tell you why and nothing my parents try to do will matter then."

"What are you talking about, Bethanie? You keep hinting at something. Just tell me what's going on."

"You're the detective. You tell me," she says like this is some kind of joke.

"Look, I want to tell you something about Cole. Is he with you now?"

"Of course he's with me, and anything you say about him I'm just going to tell him anyway, so just say it."

"It's not like that. I just want to make sure you can hear me. I don't know how you can hear anything with all that noise. Can you go somewhere a little quieter so—"

Then I hear a man's voice in the background—Cole's voice—telling her to hang up, and she does, without even saying good-bye.

Now I'm really scared for Bethanie, even if Cole did seem like a nice guy except for the gold-digging thing, and even if Bethanie says he's always a gentleman. All that can change with the quickness, especially when dealing with a con artist. Bethanie thinks she's playing out some kind of secret mission or modern-day *Romeo and Juliet* and has no idea she's creeping with the enemy.

I'm surprised to find Lana on the phone when I get inside since her car wasn't out front. She looks at me and then at her watch, but doesn't stop her conversation to ask me why I'm home from school so early. That means she's talking to someone about the case. I pretend to go to my room, but hide in the hall to eavesdrop. Most of the conversation is lame and not at all helpful, until she says, "We had the statewide BOLO out on him, so why didn't Black Hawk police apprehend him when they had a visual?"

I don't get to hear the reason why the missing witness wasn't apprehended, but then Lana says, "Well, at least we know he's probably still in Colorado, though I don't get how he's able to stay hidden so well and for so long when he's got a wife and kid in tow."

That's when it hits me. Although MJ has pretty much confirmed it was Cole in that photo and he's tied to Lana's case, I don't think he was up in Black Hawk this weekend and he definitely isn't hanging out with a wife and kid. Well, not *his* kid, anyway. I always thought Bethanie wasn't her real name. It just didn't fit her, especially after I met her mother. No way would her mom name a child of hers Bethanie. Aloe Vera or Taffy maybe, but not Bethanie. Now I realize Larsen isn't their last name, either. That was why I couldn't find anything about them when I was in Atlanta.

When the Atlanta cops were wondering how the witness had the kind of money he was dropping at the casinos, the cute detective suggested the perp had to have robbed a bank or won the sweepstakes. He was close. The perp won the lottery. And I think he just spent the weekend up in the Black Hawk casinos satisfying his 'penchant for gambling' that Detective Sanders had talked about. I burst into the living room without caring that Lana will know I was eavesdropping.

"Lana, I gotta talk to you now. I mean right now."

"Let me call you back," she says to her partner. "What is your problem, Chanti?"

"Your perp—the missing witness—when did he drop off the radar?"

"You know I shouldn't be talking about—"

"Mom, this is for real. You have to tell me. Was it right before school started?"

"Yeah, about that time."

"You've been surveilling casinos, but have you been watching other places he could gamble, like horse and dog tracks, maybe private poker games?"

"No, that's never been his MO. He only gambles in casinos—poker and blackjack."

You could play those games and more at the Black Hawk

casinos. But why would Cole be looking for him at the race-track? Not only does he know where Mr. Larsen lives, but if the cops know that isn't Mr. Larsen's modus operandi, shouldn't Cole know, too?

"His kid—a girl my age, right?"

"A year older. Chanti, have you been sneaking into my files again, because—"

"I need to see a picture of your perp."

Lana must think I'm either crazy or on to something, because after she stares at me for a second like she doesn't recognize me, she starts looking through her briefcase and pulls out a picture.

"Oh snap," I say when I see it, and my stomach starts twisting up like someone's kneading dough in there.

"What's going on, Chanti?"

"I know where you can find him."

Chapter 21

Finally I admit to myself that I have absolutely nothing under control. The minute I learned Cole was part of a crime family, I knew Bethanie was in trouble, but I didn't know how much trouble until I realized Bethanie's dad was the missing witness who was supposed to testify against the Family. That's when I decide to tell Lana everything I know. I'm showing her the out-of-focus photo of Cole that I found on her desk when I hear MJ banging on our front door. I know it's her because she keeps yelling, "Chanti, open the door!" until I do.

She looks full of news until she sees Lana sitting in the living room.

"I didn't know she was here. Her car usually be out front."

"I had to take it to the shop," Lana says. "My partner dropped me off."

"That dude I see you with sometimes is your partner?" MJ asks. "I thought that was your man."

"That's what everyone thinks. Now that I've trusted you with my biggest secrets, can you try to trust me?"

Lana's civility surprises both MJ and me.

"It's okay, MJ, I told her everything," I say to reassure her Lana isn't looking to entrap her into an arrest. MJ thinks every cop on the planet is out to get her, whether she's done anything to deserve it or not. That's the perspective you take when you go to juvie for a crime you don't feel you committed.

"Well, you know how I said Cole joined the Family and moved up real quick? Seems like it's because he got in good with the Boss in, like, zero to sixty. The rest of the Family don't like him much."

"Hating on him for moving up too fast?" I ask.

"That, and they just straight-up don't trust him. Some worry he's going after their position, but a few think he's positioning himself to be the Boss's right hand so he can take over the Family while the Boss is doing his time once your friend's father testifies against him."

"But this guy is barely out of college, right?" Lana asks.

"If we believe what he says, he's twenty-one," I say. "He looks about that. But who can trust anything he says now?"

"There's no way the Boss would let someone so young and inexperienced, not to mention distrusted by his soldiers, take over the Family," Lana says.

"But that explains why Cole is here," MJ says. "The Boss sent him after Larsen to kill him and prevent him from testifying. A kill shows your loyalty to the Family."

"Or if the rumors you're hearing are right," I suggest, "maybe Cole is going to double-cross the Boss and bring Mr. Larsen—or whatever his real name is—back alive and able to testify against him so he goes to jail and Cole takes over."

"You mean like he's working with the cops? He'd be the ultimate snitch and the Family would eighty-six him the minute they even suspected it."

"You're right, MJ," Lana says. "If Chanti's right about his plan, he's working alone. However he delivers Larsen to the cops, it won't be in a way someone could tie him to it."

Every interaction I've had with Cole, and every conversation I've had with Bethanie about him plays back in my head like I'm running it on TiVo. The car that I saw leaving Bethanie's street early that morning with its windows all frosted up—it was a silver Porsche like that cleaning crew guy at Cole's apartment had described and like I saw in the photo. Were his windows all frosted up because he'd been there overnight and had somehow sneaked into the house to be with Bethanie? I doubt it with Tiny around and with the killer security system Mr. Larsen must have now that I know who he is. That leasing agent said Cole's car had picnic stuff in the backseat. Sounds a lot like the backseat of Lana's car with all the stuff she needs for a stakeout. No, the windows were frosted over because he'd been there all night but not in Bethanie's room. He'd been staked out on the street, watching the house, probably learning the Larsens' schedule and habits, or more specifically, Bethanie's.

"He's been watching her since the bodega robbery," I say out loud without realizing it.

"What about the bodega robbery?" Lana asks, sounding like she's about to go all cop-mother on me and put me in the box. "What does your friend have to do with that?"

"Ms. Evans, I swear I don't know a thing about that robbery," MJ says, sounding guilty.

"Not you," Lana says, "the other friend. The one gone missing."

"Okay, Lana, keeping in mind we have a much bigger case to deal with here," I say, hoping she won't kill me when I tell her, "I was in the bodega when it was robbed."

"I told you to stay away from that place! And why am I just hearing about it?"

"Because I knew you'd be mad if I was there. . . ."

"Damn right I'm mad."

"And I knew you'd be even angrier when you found out I ditched before the cops got there."

"You were a witness to a crime and didn't report it?"

MJ looks at me and I just know she's thinking I'm a hypocrite because in our past dealings with the police and getting arrested, I told her it wasn't being a snitch to help them get the bad guys. *Yeah*, I'm sure she's thinking, *unless it's your own skin you're trying to save.*

"Okay, that was wrong. But soon after the robbery, I began suspecting it wasn't an actual crime. I always thought the way it went down wasn't right—how the long line for the BOGO tamales suddenly disappeared. And how Cole acted so stupid, trying to be a hero when anyone from around here knows what to do in a robbery—keep your head down and let it play out so you don't get killed. For that matter, what was Cole doing there anyway, is what I kept asking Bethanie. Tommy Hilfiger–wearing white boys just don't shop at the bodega."

"So you think he was casing her before the robbery?" Lana asks.

"I do. That's how he knew Bethanie gives me a ride home every Friday and how I always stop in the bodega for the Friday BOGO tamales."

Lana gives me an evil look for lying all this time about staying away from the bodega, but only says, "You think he set the whole robbery up so he could be there to save the day for her."

"Yeah, and he had to have some help on the inside. I didn't recognize the guy at the cash register that day," I say, staring straight at MJ.

She ignores my insinuation and asks, "What girl is stupid enough for the whole Prince Charming thing to work on her?"

"You don't know Bethanie," I tell MJ. "And aren't you the girl who spent two years in JD because your boyfriend talked you into being his getaway driver for the bank robbery?"

"I told you a million times—he said he needed a ride there so he could open his account."

"Yeah, I think you just answered your own question," I

tell MJ. "You know better than anyone how a boy can make you stupid sometimes."

She looks away from me, which only confirms her guilt and answers the question I've had since I ran into MJ outside the bodega that early morning. Eddie must have been the cashier that I didn't recognize, the one who mysteriously disappeared before the cops showed up. I want to know MJ's involvement in this whole scheme, but I won't say anything now. Even though MJ is helping us, Lana's still a cop and will take MJ in if she thinks she's got something to do with Cole's bodega setup. She does, but just like the bank robbery, she probably didn't know what Eddie was up to.

"He did it to gain her trust," I explain, letting MJ off the hook for now. "I think he needed to get her away from her family because her father pretty much had her on lockdown all the time, and then use her safe return to coerce her father to testify."

"It's a good theory, Chanti," Lana says. "What I don't get is how he knew where to find Bethanie and her family long before we did. Atlanta PD didn't figure out he might be in the Denver area until a few weeks before they asked me to get involved."

"He's probably been tailing the Larsens since they left Atlanta, which is why he was a few steps ahead of the Atlanta police."

"Like I told Chanti, the street is always way ahead of the five-o, 24/7/365," MJ says smugly.

"Does she always talk in numbers?"

"I never noticed that, but I guess she does," I say. "We'd better get moving on what we know."

"Don't think you're getting off for this bodega robbery thing, Chanti. But you're right, that can wait. I don't want to deliver this kind of information over the phone, and I need to pull Atlanta into this. Let's get down to the department so I can share this with the team."

"Well, let me know how it works out, Chanti," MJ says. "I hope your friend is okay."

"You'll learn firsthand how it works out because you're coming with us," Lana says. "I may need to use your contacts again."

"Oh no. I don't go into any police station, not unless I'm in cuffs and got no choice."

"I can do that for you if you'd like," Lana says, though I'm pretty sure she's kidding. I think. I hope she is because MJ outweighs her by forty pounds and is a few inches taller. On the other hand, Lana is a karate black belt who carries two guns on her at all times. It could get real ugly.

"I'm kidding," Lana says, apparently recognizing the tension she kicked up with her not-so-funny joke. "I can't do that unless I subpoena you as a witness, which I can do if you make me."

Okay, now we all know she isn't joking.

"Let me go tell my grandmother where I'm going."

"Call her from the car," Lana says, hustling us both out of the house.

MJ gives me a look that says she could kill me, and I'm pretty sure the next time I come knocking on her door looking for her help, she's going to pretend she isn't home.

Chapter 22

When we get to the police station, I can tell MJ is about as nervous as I'd be if we were in a building full of ex-cons. Lana takes us to her desk and tells us to wait. I take her chair behind the desk and leave the interview chair for MJ. That's the one where everyone who has to talk to Lana must sit—victims, family of victims, witnesses, and witnesses who turn out later to be the perp. It was probably a bad choice of seating because now MJ looks even more uncomfortable. I imagine she's sat in the interview chair as a member of every category, and definitely the last one.

Before Lana leaves us to find her CO, I ask, "So you're going to tell them I was really eavesdropping when I was with you at the Atlanta PD?"

"I don't need to give all the details now. I'll just tell him between what I knew of the case and some information you gave me about your friend, I put two and two together. Maybe later, after we find your friend, I can tell him my daughter is something of a detective herself."

"Then I'll get the collar, right?"

"No, I don't think so."

"I figured out the whole thing."

"You did, but you have to be a cop to get the collar."

"Oh yeah, right."

She leaves and goes to her boss's office. Then I see the two of them plus a couple of other detectives go into the strategy room. It's something like you see on TV cop shows without all the high-tech gadgets. There's no holographic table with a 3-D rendering of the suspect. There's no wall of GPS mapping with every coordinate of the perp's location based on the ESN signals of his mobile phone. There *is* a wall-sized whiteboard with a bunch of writing and photos taped to it, but that's not so impressive. We have one of those in some of the classrooms at Langdon.

I see the whiteboard wall has pictures of Mr. Larsen on it. There's even one of Bethanie and her mother, but none of Cole. Whatever his role in the crime family MJ's contact says he's part of, or however he might be connected to Mr. Larsen's case, nobody at the Atlanta PD or in Denver must think he's important enough to include in the investigation. That could be good or bad. If I can believe all the Mafia movies, he isn't "made" yet, which means he's never killed anyone—very good for Bethanie. Or if he's an ambitious sort of mobster, he might be looking to get promoted by doing something to change his status—seriously bad for my friend.

There's a glass wall facing the hallway so I can see Lana talking to her boss, then pointing at the whiteboard wall, but I can't make out what they're saying. I turn my attention to MJ, who I think might get sick all over Lana's desk any minute.

"You don't look so good."

"That's what you want to be—a cop?" MJ says, like I wanted a job kicking puppies.

"I haven't really thought of what I want to be."

"Bull. Everybody knows what they want to be, whether they have any chance of being it or not."

"So what do you want to be, then?"

"I ain't in the mood to talk about it."

The way she keeps fidgeting in the interview chair, I don't think she's in the mood to talk about *anything*. I figure since I got her into this, I should at least come clean about my career aspirations. Besides, I need something to keep my mind off Bethanie and what Cole might have done to her when he made her get off the phone so abruptly.

"I do sort of want to be a cop, but not like Lana. You have to not be afraid of everything to be that kind of cop."

"Chanti, you keep saying stuff like that, but for you to always be in some mess like this, I don't think you're as afraid of stuff as you think."

"No, Lana's kind of crime solving isn't for me. I want to be one of those forensic cops."

"Oh yeah, like on those *CSI* shows, right, 'cause you like science," MJ says like she just figured out a big mystery herself. MJ would have my back in anything, and could probably take out even the scariest boy at school, but she will never make class valedictorian.

"Now would be as good a time as any to tell me about Eddie."

"I got nothing to say about Eddie."

"Well, I'll tell you what I think and you can let me know if I'm warm. Obviously he's your boyfriend. . . ."

"He is not my boyfriend. Just a guy I like."

"Okay, he's a guy you hope will be your boyfriend, and we know your track record in letting guys get you into trouble. You had to have known him before he worked with Cole to set up the bodega robbery."

"He didn't help Cole. He didn't know who he was helping. Some dude came into the store just before tamale happy hour started and offered Eddie a thousand dollars to disappear for an hour."

"What? I saw him at the counter taking orders and ringing people up. He didn't disappear until after the robbery."

"You got it all bass-ackwards. You think Eddie was the guy in on the robbery."

"Wasn't he?"

"Sort of, but not the way you think. Eddie is the owner's son. He had just started working in the store that day."

"That's convenient," I say. Someone was lying—MJ to me or Eddie to her.

"He just got into town a couple weeks ago. He dropped out of college, so his dad told him he had to earn his keep by working in the store, or go back to school. Eddie was filling in for his cousin, the owner's nephew and the cashier you're used to seeing. His cousin hasn't had a vacation in two years and he took the chance when he got it."

"Why have I never seen or heard of Eddie until now? I go to the bodega all the time."

"You never met Eddie 'cause he's always been away at school. He and his father don't get along, so he don't come home summers."

"I can see why his father doesn't like him—he lets people rob his store," I say. "Still seems like I should know something about him."

"True, since you stay in everybody's business," MJ says. "But his father didn't buy the bodega from his brother until a couple years ago, about the same time Eddie started school. That means Eddie never lived in Denver until two weeks ago."

"So how did you know him?"

"I told you. Big Mama is friends with Eddie's father." She starts making weird faces at me then, raising her eyebrows a lot. I'm beginning to think she's lost it, but then I get it. Big Mama doesn't just *know* Eddie's father. She's running her Numbers game with him. Of course we can't say that inside the police department since running Numbers would get Big Mama arrested.

"So your grandmother is expanding the business," I say,

just to mess with MJ for holding out on me with the Eddie story.

"Would you shut up?" she whispers. More like snarls. "I met him one time when I went over there early one morning to run an errand for Big Mama."

"Wait, MJ. You aren't working for her, are you? Your probation—"

"Hell no. She wouldn't allow that. Stop thinking like a cop all the time. I really was running an errand. She sent me to get milk."

"Like that morning I ran into you on Center Street? You said you were getting milk then, too. But you didn't have any milk and you weren't dressed for the cold morning."

MJ looks like she's been busted. She definitely could never play poker because everything she's thinking always shows on her face.

"That's 'cause I wasn't picking up milk *that* morning. I didn't have a coat on because it wasn't cold when I went over there the night before."

It took me a second to figure out what she was talking about, and when I did, for some reason I turned into a ten-year-old.

"Oooh, you and Eddie were in there all night. I know what y'all were doing."

"Duh, Sherlock. I didn't plan to stay all night. You caught me trying to get back home before Big Mama got back from her overnight church trip to the Springs."

"So where is Eddie now?"

"He's still here, but he's thinking of going back to school. He's afraid his pops is going to find out how he gave up the store on his first day on the job so it could be used for a fake robbery."

"Yeah, not too bright," I say, thinking MJ really knows how to pick 'em.

"He didn't know the guy was going to stage a robbery."

That reminds me of what Lana said about the store being empty when the cops arrived and no money being missing.

"How exactly did he know that's what happened? There were no security cameras, no witnesses."

"Eddie waited in the back parking lot for the part-time lady who helps with the Freebie rush. He met her at the back door and told her she had a paid day off. Eddie left after that, but didn't stay away the whole hour. He got worried what the guy was up to and crept in the back way, got there just as it was going down."

"I had a feeling someone was in the back. I thought I smelled food cooking."

"Yeah, that's another reason Eddie came back. His mom makes the tamales in the morning so all the afternoon clerks have to do is keep them warm. He remembered he'd left some tamales in the warmer and was worried he'd burn the place down."

Wow, this guy might actually be worse than her last boyfriend.

"He was in the back when the cops arrived. He went out front before the cops searched the store. Told them he'd just stepped out back for a minute to take a smoke and there was no way a robbery had gone down in that short amount of time—it must have been a prank call. When he checked the register and nothing was missing, the cops believed him and left."

"So the cashier was the guy who made the deal with Eddie to leave the store?"

"Yeah. It was a thousand dollars, Chanti."

"He could have wiped the store out. I'm sure Eddie's father would agree the contents of the store was worth a lot more than a thousand dollars."

"I suppose. Yet another reason Eddie will probably go back to school before his father finds out."

"No, I'll bet he'll stick around either way," I say.

"You think?" MJ says, and smiles for the first time since she walked into Lana's office.

From what little I know of Eddie's intellectual prowess, I don't think he left school on his own accord, but I don't mention this to MJ. I'll let her go on thinking she found a good catch, at least for now. We've got to save Bethanie first.

Chapter 23

A minute later, Lana comes out of the strategy room toward us.

"Don't tell her," MJ whispers.

"Not now. But at some point, we'll need Eddie to ID Cole as the guy who offered him a thousand dollars."

"We got a little more information on Cole," Lana says when she reaches us, "but it only confirms what you learned from your contacts, MJ. He's a low-level foot soldier in the Family trying hard to move up and get made quickly. The fastest way to do that is to make a kill."

Now I feel as sick as MJ looked when we first arrived. "But why Bethanie? Why not her dad?"

"We still think her dad is the target. Wait here a minute while we get a team together to go bring in her family."

"Damn," MJ says when Lana leaves. "It's looking bad for your girl, no matter what your mom thinks."

"She thinks the same thing we do. She just said that so I won't freak out."

"So we need to figure out why Cole would want your friend instead of her father 'cause we know that's why they sent him out here. Once we know that, we come up with the plan to find him, right?"

"Right."

"And you have a theory, the one you explained back at your house. He'll use Bethanie as ransom to make her pops turn himself in to the police."

"Ransom. That's it, MJ."

"That's what?"

"I just came up with another theory. Cole came out here to kill Mr. Larsen, found out he won the Powerball—"

"Wow. You didn't say they were that rich. That explains a whole helluva lot, then."

"But not everything. Powerball money still won't keep the Boss out of jail, which is why Cole was sent. Maybe he figured he could get the money *and* kill Mr. Larsen, so he's holding Bethanie ransom."

"But that won't help him take over the Family like my contacts told me was the word on the street," MJ reminds me.

"True."

"Maybe he's like Donnell. Remember how he was going to rob your boss and use the money to start up his own Down Homes operation in Denver? Could be Cole is doing the same thing—using your friend to make Larsen testify *and* set him up with bank so he can go back and take over the business. He can buy a lot of friends in the Family with that kind of money."

"That's brilliant, MJ."

She's no Rhodes scholar but when it comes to criminal minds, MJ is Stephen Hawking smart.

I notice MJ looks a lot less worried about being in the interview chair. Maybe that's the secret to getting her to see cops aren't all bad—letting her be on the same team. I'm about to offer her my seat when I see Lana through the window of the strategy room waving us over. Right away, MJ looks nervous again.

"Relax, MJ, we aren't the ones in trouble this time," I tell her.

When we get into the room, Lana introduces us to the detectives.

"It's okay, guys. I told my CO everything. I had to, there was no way around it."

"Young ladies, this is quite some detective work you're doing here. We want you on our team, but first we need to talk about confidentiality."

"You can trust Chanti. She's protected my cover as well as any partner would," Lana says, which would make me grin like a fool if I wasn't sick with worry over Bethanie.

"I don't doubt it. But I understand you have a history, Miss Cooper."

"Ancient history," MJ says in her tone that warns people to back down or a butt-kicking is about to ensue. Luckily, Lana steps in.

"I trust MJ equally," she says, surprising us both. "She helped us with that burglary ring last month and saved Chanti's life in the process."

Her boss accepts Lana's word on MJ and I but still makes us sign some kind of form saying we have to keep police secrets. It's second nature for me to keep secrets since I know how important it is to Lana's safety, and someone would have to torture MJ to make her ever admit to helping the cops. Right now she's probably just as worried about her street cred as getting Bethanie out of trouble, maybe more. Even though she's given up the life, not everything goes away.

"Tell me about that phone call you had with Bethanie," Lana says, checking her watch. "It's been about an hour, right?"

I know she's asking for the time because the clock has begun to tick. If Cole made her get off the phone because he's worried someone's onto him, common cop wisdom is that we only have twenty-four hours to find her. That's the magic hour when things start to go bad for a hostage, even if she doesn't realize that's what she is.

"It sounded like she was at an amusement park when I called her."

"This late in October?"

"I guess she's not in the state."

"Could it have been a video arcade?"

"A what?" MJ asks.

"Whatever you kids call them now, like Dave and Buster's."

"No one but little kids and old people go there," MJ says. "Well, not real old, but like your age."

Lana frowns at that statement.

"It didn't sound like that. It was more like the sounds of one of those traveling carnivals that set up in parking lots for a couple of weeks in the summer. The kind you wouldn't let me go to when I was a kid because you thought they weren't regulated enough."

"If she's in the country, that doesn't leave much. Florida, maybe Southern California," Lana says. "It's getting too cold everywhere else to run an amusement park."

"You think they might not even be in the country?" I ask.

"It's something we have to consider. But first I'll check on amusement parks open this time of year. Anything else?"

"She kept saying she was so happy and excited to tell me why, and how her parents wouldn't be able to tell her what to do anymore."

"Any ideas what was making her so happy?"

I couldn't tell Lana that it might be because she and Cole had finally done the deed after she'd been trying to seduce him for a couple of weeks, so I told her I didn't have any idea because it was true. I'm pretty sure there's something else going on besides losing her virginity.

After MJ and I share our newest theories with Lana and the rest of the team, they work on revising their strategy to bring in Mr. Larsen. In the meantime, they tell me to look through some of the surveillance photos to see if I recognize anyone else in them like I did with Cole. They show MJ to an office where she can make a call to her Atlanta Homies to see if they might have any more information. I imagine MJ must be breaking out in hives right about now, having to call her ex-gang members from a police department, even if it's from her cell phone and they'd never know. Unless they have one of those GPS tracking wall grids like on TV. I'm guessing a low-rent gang called the Down Homes probably doesn't, but that didn't keep MJ from looking like she was going to the gallows when she left the strategy room.

I'm looking through some surveillance photos taken of the Family when I come across some of a wedding. The way the Boss is smiling, I'm guessing it's his daughter, and that's confirmed when I see more photos of them together. I know I watch too much TV, but I wonder if he's happy for his daughter or if her marriage just made him more powerful because her new husband is also part of a crime family. See how my mind wanders, even at a time like this? For all I know her husband could be a schoolteacher or a bank teller. From what I can tell, it doesn't matter to the new bride what her husband does for a living because she looks so happy, like she doesn't have a care in the world even though her family is a bunch of criminals.

Is love what it takes to make you not care about who a guy really is, or if you do know, to still not care? From the little Lana has told me about my father, that's how I came to be. She hooked up with someone she knew she shouldn't have. Isn't that exactly what MJ did when she became her boyfriend's getaway driver? She even told me that's why she joined the Down Homes in the first place—because the boy she loved was a member. It's the very reason—or excuse, Tasha would say—that I never had a boyfriend before Marco. I don't want to ever be so stupid over a guy that I lose my mind and good sense. What if Bethanie is that stupid crazy about Cole? Worse, what if she knows what he's about and is going along, like those people with Stockholm Syndrome?

Something about thinking the Boss's daughter could be marrying a bank teller, a counter of money, plus Cole's fascination with having Bethanie teaching him how to gamble, and the sounds I heard in the background during Bethanie's calls give me an idea. My TV addiction helps me come up with the idea, too.

"Lana," I yell too loudly because she and her team are just at the next table over. "I need to see some surveillance tape of one of the casinos."

"Okay, wait a minute and I'll—"

"Really. I need to see them now."

Lana's boss looks at her like *You raised this unruly kid?* but Lana knows I'd never talk to her like that unless it was do or die and I was really onto a clue. She ignores her boss and walks over to the TV and puts in a DVD.

"Is it muted? I need audio."

Lana turns up the volume and now I know for sure.

"That's the sound I heard. They weren't at an amusement park when Bethanie called. She was calling from inside a casino. A Las Vegas casino."

"How do you know it's Las Vegas? Could be Black Hawk. He may have gone up there looking for Larsen."

"Because that's how Cole got her to go with him without a fight. That's why instead of being terrified, she's acting like being kidnapped by a Mafia dude is just the bestest thing in the world. He told her they'd elope to Vegas and she was crazy enough, or in love enough, to believe him."

Chapter 24

On the drive to the Larsens, I imagine what I'll say to them but come up with nothing. What do you say when you're part of the reason someone's kid has gone missing? I mean, that's how they'll see it even if I tell them Bethanie was leaving with Cole without my help and at least this way we're still in contact with her. That's why Lana tells me to wait in the car while she and her partner tell the Larsens what's going on, and then she'll come out and get me when she thinks it's okay. Maybe if MJ had come along with us instead of staying back at the department I'd have stayed in the car. But she didn't and I don't. The minute I see Lana get inside the house, I follow.

I'm in luck; they left the door unlocked. I'm just inside the foyer so I can hear everything but they can't see me. Unfortunately I can't see them either, so I just have voices to go on to tell who is there.

"I know why y'all here, and I never thought I'd say it but I'm almost relieved," Mr. Larsen says.

"How do you know? Have you made contact?" Lana asks.

"No, but I gotta feeling it won't be long and I'd rather it be y'all calling than them."

"Mr. Larsen, I think there's some confusion here."

"I'm not confused. Y'all here to take me into protective custody."

"We should never have run in the first place," Mrs. Larsen says.

"Yeah, right, Lola Mae. That ain't what you said when we went down there to cash in that ticket," Mr. Larsen says.

"You want to let us in on the secret?" Lana asks.

Mr. Larsen lets out a big sigh, like he's thinking he might as well just come clean. "The Sunday before the police told us about the deal to testify against DeLong, me and Mama had bought us a Powerball ticket. When that ticket turned out to have the winning numbers on Wednesday, we decided we didn't need no help from the police. With all that money, we could go into our own protective custody—change our names, get out of town, live on cash. No one can track you if you never have a job and pay everything in cash."

"So you thought," says Mrs. Larsen. "The cops found us, and they ain't the only ones."

"You think DeLong has found you, too?" That's Detective Falcone, Lana's partner. I'm guessing DeLong must be the guy they've been calling the Boss this whole time.

"I think somebody is on our tail and it ain't the cops. A week ago, I spotted a car out front, one house down, early on a Sunday morning. Folks around here use their garages, and this car had been parked outside all night. The windows were all frosted over."

Score one for me. That *was* Cole watching the house that morning I went to see Bethanie.

"Then here come another car pull up in front of my house," Mr. Larsen continues. "A man gets out but soon as he notices the car with the frosted windows, he gets back in his car and takes off. That's when I run down to see if I can tail him. By the time I get out the garage, the car that had been there all night was gone, too."

Take my point away. I didn't realize that first car I saw leaving Bethanie's street was part of this story and didn't pay attention to what it looked like. In my defense, it was really cold that morning and I was just trying to get someplace warm.

"Did you catch up with them?" Lana asks.

"Naw, I lost 'em."

"That's probably a good thing. These guys are dangerous," Falcone says. "How about a plate?"

"No plate, but I can describe both cars. The one what was here all night was a silver Porsche. The guy he scared off was driving a blue Jag."

Bethanie told me the guy waiting for her in her favorite parking spot that day was driving a Jag. Cole scared him off that day, too. At the time, I doubted how preppie Cole could scare off a serious thug but clearly I underestimated him. How could I know he was the right-hand man of a crime family boss? Now I'm wondering why this guy in the Jag keeps showing up, and why Cole has to keep running him off.

"Then there's a boy been sniffin' around my daughter. First I thought he was just some con artist after the money. That's one place we went wrong. It's hard when you never had nothing to keep pretending like you still don't have nothing after you win all that money. Could be we was a little too flashy with our newfound wealth."

"Yes, I can imagine." I bet Lana's looking around at Mrs. Larsen's interior design choices right now. "What made you think he might be after something more than money?"

"Can't say exactly. When you been in my trade for as long as I have . . ."

"You mean hustling?"

"I like to call it entrepreneuring. Anyway, I've been around enough cons to get a sense of it. I never met this boy, I only know his name is Cole, but the way he pulled my daughter into his confidence so quick made me worried."

"Well, that brings us to why we're here. It isn't exactly for the reason you think, I'm afraid," Falcone says. "We came about your daughter."

"She oughtta be here by now. She stayed the weekend with a school friend of hers while we were up in the mountains taking in the scenery."

"You mean the poker tables, don't you?" says Mrs. Larsen. "Boringest place I ever been to. Didn't even have nowhere to shop, did they, Josephine?"

I'm wondering who Josephine could be until I hear the person they've been calling Molly, the maid, answer in agreement. I knew that was a fake name, just like Tiny and the Larsens.

"Truth is, we starting to get worried 'cause she's a couple hours late," says Mr. Larsen. "But soon as she gets home, we'll all go with y'all wherever we need to go to get that protective custody. I'm tired of looking over my shoulder."

"We get to keep the lottery money, right?" Mrs. Larsen asks.

I can't stand waiting in that foyer another minute listening to the Larsens and their belief that Bethanie is coming through the door any minute, so I come out of hiding. Mrs. Larsen sees me first.

"Chantal, where you come from? This here is the girl Bethanie stayed with over the weekend. Did Bethanie go upstairs without even coming in to see us? These kids and their manners," she says to Lana.

Lana looks at me and I shake my head. I should be the one to tell them, at least that's what I thought when I stepped into the living room. But now I can't make the words come. They're all just staring at me, waiting, expecting some explanation, but then I see in Mrs. Larsen's eyes that she is slowly figuring out something is wrong. Mr. Larsen is, too, and stands up as if that will make everything clear to him. Lana takes over and I'm relieved.

"Please, sit down. Unfortunately, you were right to suspect this young man. We think he was the driver of that silver Porsche and that he was indeed watching your house, probably for some time."

"I knew we should have hired some real protection 'stead of your cousin Tiny," Mrs. Larsen says. "Always so cheap. A real bodyguard would have noticed somebody casing us all that time."

"Mr. and Mrs. Larsen, that's not all of it," Lana says, and pauses a second before she continues. "We believe your daughter has left town with him."

"Lord have mercy," both Larsens say at the same time.

"The good news is we believe she's well, and in fact, she may have gone with him willingly."

"Why would she do that?" Mrs. Larsen asks.

Now it really is my turn to speak up.

"If I could take a look around, mainly in her room, I might find some clues to where Bethanie might be."

"You won't be looking around nowhere. Why you need clues to tell me my child spent the whole weekend with you?" Mrs. Larsen says, each word getting higher pitched than the one before it, reminding me of Squeak.

"Because she didn't really stay with me over the weekend. I was just . . . I covered for her because she wanted to be with Cole."

"You helped this boy kidnap my child?" Mrs. Larsen looks at me like she might come over and strangle me where I stand, and I almost can't blame her.

I can tell Lana is trying to figure out if she should blow her cover even more than she already has just by being here as a cop and not undercover, and let them know she's also my mother.

"We sent her over to your place thinking you might talk some sense into her about this boy, and you help him steal her away from us?"

I don't know any other way to say it than to just say it, so I do. "She was going with him whether I helped or not. She was always saying she never got to be a regular girl, always on lockdown, never having a boyfriend, because . . . well, she said you were very overprotective, Mr. Larsen. She never told me why, and once I figured out you won the Powerball, I thought it was about your money."

Mr. Larsen looks stunned. "You knew about the money?"

"Not because she told me. I figured it out myself. She was always protective of you, too, even when I tried to get her to tell me what was going on. Then I realized this goes back to long before the money came along. I mean, she'll be seventeen in a couple of days and never had a boyfriend or even a real date, but with her looks, boys are always coming on to her. My experience—my mother's line of work—made me suspect your being so guarded over Bethanie had something to do with what you did for a living, which I also knew had nothing to do with the oil business."

"What all this got to do with you helping my child's kidnapper? Shouldn't we be out looking for them? I ain't got time to listen to this child tell me what I did wrong as a parent."

"What Chanti is trying to say will make sense in a minute, but it's important."

"What you know about her?" Mrs. Larsen asks Lana. "She's just some girl over at that rich school on a scholarship. Here I thought I was protecting Bethanie from the wrong element and I'm sending her right into the wolves."

"I know her because she's my daughter."

"What the hell is going on?" Mr. Larsen asks. "Nothing I heard so far makes a damn bit of sense."

Lana gives the Larsens a quick rundown on how I got to be involved in their case, and ends by telling them to trust me because I'm a good detective, too, even if no one's paying me for the job. So I finish what I was trying to tell them.

"You had Bethanie on such a tight leash, overprotective was an understatement. I know from Lana's work that usually only cops and criminals are that paranoid. I knew you weren't a cop, and I didn't get the feeling you were a criminal, either, but you probably associated with some. Then when I suggested Cole was after your money, you seemed relieved. That meant you were afraid he was capable of much worse than being a con artist. I connected that with your gambling habit and I figured you owed some scary people a lot of money, and probably on the regular. When I learned about Lana's case, I just put it all together. There were lots of other clues, but that doesn't matter now."

Both Larsens look deflated. Before they were angry and ready to kick butt—mine, Cole's. Now they look angry and scared.

"So she went away with this boy to get back at me for protecting her?"

"Some of it to get back at you, but a lot of it because she's in love."

"What's a girl who never been on a date know about love?" Mr. Larsen asks.

His wife gives him an answer. "That's why she fell so easy. We did wrong, keeping her apart from things every girl should have."

"It was wrong that I lied and covered for her, but I did it for what I thought was a good reason. She was going to be with him anyway, but at least I'd be in contact with her. I never guessed she'd run off with him."

"You spoke to her today?" Mrs. Larsen asks.

"I did, and at this point I think she has no idea Cole was sent by the Boss. She actually sounded very happy when we spoke."

"But now we're working against a clock," Lana says. "I'm surprised he hasn't contacted you yet. Chanti thinks he may have told her some *Romeo and Juliet* story to make her leave with him, but that he really has kidnapped her. He wants something in return for her."

"What—money?"

"I have a few theories on that. Money to pay back the Boss what you owe him, plus a lot of interest. Your word that you won't testify against the Boss. Or maybe he wants to force you to testify so the Boss goes to jail and he takes over the Family."

"A punk kid like that? He could never take over the Family because—"

Mrs. Larsen cuts her husband off. "We'll do it, give him the money, turn ourselves in to the cops. I'll trade myself for her, whatever we need to do."

"You might have to do all of the above at some point but right now I just need you to let me walk through the house," I say. And without waiting for an answer, I leave the room.

Chapter 25

I'm only in the next room and can hear them. Everything is starting to sink in for the Larsens and they sound angry again.

"I'm sorry, I just can't believe Bethanie would go with some boy she don't half know unless she was forced," Mr. Larsen is saying.

"Chanti tells me that Cole can be quite charming," Lana says. "She sensed something was off about Cole the first time she met him, but even now she doesn't think he'll hurt your daughter."

"How would she know what he'll do? And why the hell is she touring my house when we should be out looking for my kid?"

"That's what we've been trying to explain. Chanti has a theory about where Bethanie and Cole might be, and it's a good one," Lana says, defending me. "It's the strongest lead we have right now. She wants to find your daughter, too."

"Well, that's very touching but I still don't understand why we just sitting here while she traipses all over my house. For that matter, I don't even understand why a child, the very child who helped Bethanie in whatever game she's playing, is even here." Each of Mrs. Larsen's words sound a little more frantic than the last, and I wonder if my being here is such a good idea.

"Believe me, I'm so angry with my daughter for her part in this that I might help you teach her a lesson, but right now, we need to find your child, and Chanti is our best chance for that."

"How? She ain't but a child herself."

"She has the gift of observation. Chanti sees things in people or places that most of us miss. It's a big part of detective work, and even though she's a kid, she's good at it. Plus, she knows Bethanie. You know how girls are at this age. Mom is the enemy. They don't want us to know anything about their very important lives."

I imagine Mrs. Larsen smiles a little at that last comment. I wish I was as good at this part as Lana is. There's more to being a detective than observing everything. You have to know how to be comfortable around people, make them believe you understand what they feel, make them trust you and give up secrets. It's the part I'm still trying to learn.

Lana sees an opening and keeps going. "I bet you there are mothers up and down this street who wish they knew more about what's going on in their daughters' lives, and not because they haven't tried. God knows we try."

"I do try. She just won't let me in. I see now how little I know about that girl these days."

"That's what Chantal gives us."

"Well, I guess that makes sense."

"Did Bethanie tell you Chantal helped us take down a burglary ring at school last month? I think she'll be a big help to us finding your daughter."

I don't hear what is said next because there's nothing in the dining room or den that gives any clues about Bethanie. I go upstairs to her room because there must be something there that might confirm Bethanie and Cole went to Las Vegas. I've only ever been in her room twice and never because she invited me in. Both times her mother told me to go up and both times Bethanie seemed angry at her mother for letting me invade. She was always trying to hide something. So far I've figured out her secrets in bits and pieces—the lottery money, her family not being who they say they are, her father being on the run from both the bad guys and the good guys—but I'm pretty sure I still don't know everything.

She never hid her romance with Cole from me like she did all the other secrets. Either she had nothing to hide, or by the time Cole came along she knew a lot more about my gift, as Lana calls it, and decided it was better to let me think she was telling me everything. Mrs. Larsen said she already looked through Bethanie's room and didn't find anything strange. That's not a surprise. Most moms don't know everything even when they think they do. I even manage to keep a few secrets from supercop Lana. In Bethanie's case, her parents are completely clueless, almost like they don't even know their daughter, much less her secrets.

I should be able to find clues her mother would never find in a million years but will jump out at me, lit up in neon. She would never bring Cole up here, even when her parents were away over the weekend, since Molly and Tiny live here. Tiny may not be very good at surveillance, but he would scare any guy off, maybe even one sent to kill a witness for his boss. When they were together while I was covering for them, it was not in this room. But that isn't the kind of clue I'm looking for.

There aren't too many books on her bookshelf, and the few there are all math books, books about probability and statistics. I knew she was a math genius but it's weird that she'd have all these books because she never seemed to like math very much. I figured it was something she came by naturally, like the way I can see things other people can't. I open one of the books and it has a bunch of sticky notes in handwriting that doesn't belong to Bethanie. Probably a man's handwriting.

The notes look a lot like homework assignments, telling someone—Bethanie, I suppose—what to study. I put it back on the shelf. One book seems really out of place, a big book of fairy tales that she probably had since she was a little kid. Unlike the math books, it looks ancient and worn.

I take it off the shelf, put it on the table and let it fall open on its own. There I find a list in Bethanie's handwriting. It looks like a bucket list—all the things people want to do before they die. At the top of the sheet, she's written: *Things I Want to Do Before I'm Too Old for It to Matter.*

1. buy an Easy-Bake oven (That one is checked off.)
2. ride a roller coaster
3. have a sleepover
4. stay somewhere long enough to make friends I can invite to a sleepover
5. be the popular girl at school
6. have a birthday party with people other than my parents present
7. go to the circus
8. learn to ride a bike
9. kiss a boy
10. fall in love (That one is checked off, too.)

I was wrong. It isn't like a bucket list, it's the reverse of it. Almost everything on it is ordinary, things most girls have done long before they're about to turn seventeen. It's more like a list of things to do to create a life you haven't had a chance to live yet, and it tells me so much more about Bethanie than she could tell me herself.

Chapter 26

When I return to the living room, everyone looks eager to see me, even the Larsens. The last few minutes must have been tense in here, even if no one said a word.

"Find anything?" Lana asks.

"No, not really. But I was wondering something, Mr. Larsen. I'm guessing this isn't the first time you've had to outrun some bad debts."

"I don't need a child judging my ways right now."

"Believe me, I'm not judging," I say, which is a little bit of a lie. "Do you move around a lot?"

"I wouldn't say a lot. . . ."

"How many times would you say Bethanie has been the new girl at school?"

I really didn't need his answer, because I already know it was a lot of times. When Bethanie and I started at Langdon, we began in the eleventh grade at a school where everyone is required to start in ninth. I was completely stressed about being the new girl. Bethanie didn't like the concept either, but she adapted more quickly than I did. She even started hanging with the It Girl before I squashed her Langdon career with a little detective work. Now I realize Bethanie was a pro at being the new girl.

"This time was going to be different," Mr. Larsen says, answering my question without really answering. "We had the money, no one knew where we were. She was going to start and finish a school year in the same school like she always wanted. She was to be at that fancy Langdon Prep until she graduated."

"One thing Bethanie told me about the time she's been spending with Cole seemed weird to me. He kept asking her to teach him how to play poker, and how she might use her math genius to win at cards. Then I notice she has all these books upstairs about probability and statistics, little notes stuck on the pages showing her what to study."

"You think that's what this boy wants from her—to help him cheat DeLong at his own card games?"

"Interesting theory. You left the notes in those books, Mr. Larsen. Why?"

"I'm starting to feel like I'm being interrogated," he says to Lana. "Why don't you go find my child and take this girl out of here. She ain't nothing but an accomplice to this boy Cole."

"Where are you going with this, Chanti?" Lana asks.

"Did DeLong find out you were cheating him and using Bethanie to do it?"

"You must be crazy. . . ."

"The police think DeLong was after you before you left Atlanta because you didn't make good on your sports bets, and that he's after you now to keep you from testifying. And all that's true, but there's more to it than that."

"Get this girl out of my sight before you have to arrest me for something other than fleeing the law," Mr. Larsen says as he jumps from his chair.

Lana jumps up at the same time and looks at Falcone, who's been standing between the Larsens and the foyer entrance the whole time. He instinctively moves his hand to his sidearm.

"Don't be stupid, Larsen," Lana warns. "Two more detective cars have rolled up since we got here, and I expect a couple of US Marshals have joined them by now."

I take a look out the window and see that Lana is right about the backup. Not only have they arrived, but they have Tiny facedown on the lawn trying to cuff him. From the looks of it, he's resisting arrest—unsuccessfully.

Mr. Larsen sinks to his chair. "That's why DeLong took her, isn't it? He thinks Bethanie cheated him."

"He thinks *you* cheated him, but he probably knows you used Bethanie to do it," I say, and yeah, I probably sound more than a little judgmental now. "I'm guessing you have to move so often because DeLong isn't the first person you cheated. What I can't figure out is how you do it."

"DeLong ran these private parties in Atlanta, illegal casinos. I always took E with me," he explains, forgetting to use Bethanie's alias. I guess he figures it's pointless now. "We had a system of signals so we could communicate. She'd count cards when I played blackjack, and figured the probability of cards played versus cards in the deck when I played poker."

"DeLong let her join the games?" Lana asks.

"No, she sat off to the side of my table. It was easier when she was younger. People just figured I was too lazy to find a babysitter, and she'd bring some toy and pretend to play when she was really watching the cards."

"So you've been running this hustle long before Atlanta," I say. "And as soon as someone started to catch on to your scam, you had to leave town."

"It got harder to pull off as E got older. I told players she was younger than she really was, or made up excuses like she had an illness that required constant supervision. When she was a kid, she was really into it, like we had this secret mission between us. I thought she liked the cards, and hanging out with me."

"She thought that was the only way you'd pay attention

to her," I say, "so she probably did enjoy it at first. At some point, she just wanted to be a regular girl who went to the same school long enough to make friends, have a boyfriend, go on a date."

"You right, I see it now. Her being mad at me was probably what made her less careful with the signals. DeLong figured it out one night. It was the first time we'd ever been caught outright. I'd always managed to get out of town before anyone put two and two together."

"What did DeLong do when he found out?" Lana asks.

"He let us go that night, saying I had two days to give him back every cent I ever cheated him of. Thought I'd caught a lucky break and started to take my usual steps to get us out of town before his deadline, but he'd been watching us, knew our routines. The next morning, before we could leave town, E went for a run."

"I never knew she was a runner," I say, though I don't know why since it's the least important thing he's said so far. There's so much I didn't know about Bethanie, and now I'm finding I knew even less than I thought.

"Oh yeah, she got awards and medals in track and field at a couple of those schools. Running was her favorite thing, until that morning. Now she never runs."

So those awards in her room weren't only for math bowls.

"What happened that morning?" Falcone asks. He's relaxed enough that his hand is no longer hovering near his holster.

"One of DeLong's men grabbed her."

Mrs. Larsen lets out a little sound, maybe the sound of guilt for letting her husband use Bethanie for years, and the whole feeling in the room changes. I remember Bethanie's words: *You don't know nothing about me or where I come from. I can tell you now—I'm never going back.*

Mr. Larsen must sense the change, too, because he's quick

to add, "DeLong didn't hurt her, just held her for a day to let me know he meant business."

"You mean he didn't physically harm her," Lana says, looking over at me. "She must have been terrified."

"Soon as he released her, I went straight to the cops, offered to testify against him in exchange for witness protection."

Mr. Larsen says this like it should pardon him from everything else he did. What I'm hoping will happen is Lana will go upside his head with the collapsible baton she keeps hidden in an ankle holster.

But the baton stays hidden, and Lana just says, "If you were suddenly so concerned for your daughter's well-being, why didn't you follow through with the testimony and take the protection?"

"I thought we could hide ourselves with all that lottery money."

"We could have," Mrs. Larsen finally speaks, "if you hadn't started gambling again. You know these crime families have eyes all over the place, in all the casinos."

I look at Lana. So do the police.

"I don't think the Family had eyes in the casinos," I say. "They probably figured you needed your gambling fix but weren't crazy enough to try that, which is why Cole was looking for you at racetracks and OTB windows."

"Why he need to look for me anywhere if he's been watching the house?"

"True," I say, stumped when I was on such a roll. I hate that.

Lana says, "That doesn't matter now. He's kidnapped her again and this time it isn't just to send a message. Chanti, I think you're right about the ransom," Lana says.

"But why does Cole want Bethanie to teach him card games?" I ask.

"If you're right about where they might be right now, maybe he plans to fill his time waiting for his orders from DeLong by making money the way Larsen did. Or he thinks by pushing this poker and math thing with Bethanie, he'll get her to open up about it, admit she helped her father cheat DeLong."

"Why does he need to do that? Her father just said they already know he did."

"Cole is trying to get made quickly in the Family, but we know he's a rookie. You didn't get the feeling Cole could hurt Bethanie. Maybe this is more difficult for him than he imagined. Maybe he needs confirmation, to hear the evidence for himself."

"Justification before he . . ." I can't even finish the thought.

"Maybe it *is* just the ransom theory, Chanti," Lana says, remembering she isn't talking to a cop no matter how good a detective I am.

"So why hasn't he contacted me to make his demands?" Mr. Larsen asks.

"It's all the more reason we need to get moving with our plan. Chanti still has Bethanie's trust, though we believe it may now become more difficult to communicate with her because Cole is growing suspicious," Lana explains. "Bethanie doesn't know I'm a cop, but she's aware Chanti helped the police bring down that burglary ring. She's probably told Cole that Chanti is a bit of a snoop."

"No one DeLong would send out to get me would be afraid of a little girl."

"Probably not, but he won't take the chance that Bethanie will inadvertently give Chanti clues about where they are. He'll probably prevent any more contact between them. Lucky for us, Chanti already has a good idea where they are. We're going to follow her hunch since it's the best lead we have. We're going to Las Vegas, hopefully to bring your daughter home."

Chapter 27

While we kill time working on MJ's bio homework and watching a *Murder, She Wrote* marathon until Lana comes back to the hotel room, I try to convince MJ she made the right decision coming with Lana and me to Vegas. With most people, I can run a con as well as any professional, but MJ isn't buying my story.

"You know how I feel about snitching. Now I'm working with the cops? If the Homies ever found out . . ."

"How would they?"

"The only reason you and the cops are here is because of information I got from the Homies."

MJ gets up to look in the minibar refrigerator for the umpteenth time. It's killing her that Coke and Oreos are just there for the taking—well, for six dollars each—and she can't touch them. Lana swore us off the minibar.

"I would have figured it out eventually. Your information just helped speed things up. And that's what we'll say if it ever came out you helped, which it never will."

"Don't see why I needed to be here, anyway. Ever heard of the telephone?"

"They don't want to talk about this over the phone."

"Please—cops don't use phones?"

"It isn't just the cops. The feds are working on this," I say, which I shouldn't have.

"Just call your mother and have her shoot me now," she says, slamming the little refrigerator door closed. "Might as well die at the hand of someone I know."

"You aren't going to die. Not by a Vegas Homie sneaking up on you, anyway."

"How then? You know something I don't?"

See, this is what I mean about not being good with the people part of detective work. I never seem to say the right thing. Most times the truth works, so I give it a try.

"You're not here because the phone lines might be tapped or because the feds asked for you. I wanted you to come because I'm afraid to do this. Lana thinks I can help her get Cole, talk Bethanie into meeting me and get her in a position for the cops to rescue her. I'm a thinker. The very thought of getting that close to the actual thing going down makes me want to puke."

"So you want me here to have your back."

"Yeah."

"You could've just said that from the beginning."

"No one likes to admit they're a wuss."

"You do. You're always saying that, how you're afraid. But seriously, you're kind of badass and don't even know it."

"Yeah, right."

"You took down a burglary ring. A thug pulled a gun on you but you're here to tell about it. Now you're helping the cops find a fugitive witness and you're about to save your friend from a mob hit man. I'm sorry, but all that is way badass."

We're both quiet for a few minutes, watching Jessica Fletcher nab yet another killer in Cabot Cove, because we don't know what to say after such a Hallmark moment. Well, I don't imagine Hallmark would have a moment that involved a mob hit man and gangsters pulling nine millimeters, but our version does and it's just kind of awkward. While MJ flips around the channels, I take a look at the magazines on the coffee table. From the looks of them, all there is to do in Las Vegas is gamble, shop, and eat. I imagine it would be smart to do them in reverse order though; the people who gamble first probably don't have any money left to do the other two.

When I land on a full page ad for our hotel, I realize I've sent Lana and her team to stake out the wrong place. Based on the noise in the background when Bethanie called me and what I read on her reverse bucket list, my best guess was she told Cole she wanted to stay at Circus Circus, still trying to do all the things she never got to do as a kid when her father was dragging her around to illegal card games. Her parents had confirmed for me that she still hadn't been to the circus that they knew of (or the zoo, or Disney on Ice—not that I'm being judgmental), but I'd never asked them if she'd been to an amusement park. Given their track record, I'm thinking it isn't a stretch to say she hasn't.

"Bethanie's not at the Circus Circus hotel."

"So why'd you tell your mom she was?"

"Because I just figured it out."

"Where is she, then?"

"Right here, same place we are. See?" I say, showing her the ad. "There's a roller coaster inside this building. Who would have thought you could put a roller coaster inside a building?"

"I guess if they can build the Eiffel Tower, the Statue of Liberty, and the pyramids all on one street, they could put a roller coaster inside a building."

"Come on, MJ. We have to go."

"Go where? I'm about to eat those Oreos and I don't care what your mom says."

"I'll buy you a whole box of Oreos downstairs. We need to find Bethanie and Cole."

MJ looks at me like I've lost it, but she follows me out the door.

"So what are we gonna do if they're here? It's not like we can knock on two thousand doors."

"It's better than sitting in our room. There's pretty much no chance of seeing them in there. We'll call Lana, she'll get some of the team moved over here, and in the meantime, we'll watch the lobby."

Soon as we get off the elevator on the main floor, I see how stupid my plan is. First, there is more than one way to get into the hotel and we can't watch them both. Second, I think every tourist in Las Vegas is probably walking around in the main lobby alone. MJ and I sit down next to some plants and a waterfall and I give Lana a call. Once she and some more cops get here, my plan will be a lot more effective.

"What did she say?" MJ asks when I end our call.

"She'll be here in about fifteen minutes. They're going to leave a detail at the other hotel, but she said we have to follow any lead."

"So we just wait here for her?"

"Don't be so nervous. The police aren't looking for you, remember?"

"Right. It's just a habit. When I hear the cops are coming, I'm used to running, not waiting around to give 'em a tour."

Even though it's nearly impossible to pick someone out of the hordes, I give it a try. MJ is pretty useless in helping me because she's never seen Cole or Bethanie except in photos, which is never the same as knowing someone for real. Especially in this crowd.

"So how many are coming? That will be a lot of doors to knock on."

"She's bringing a subpoena to make management show her the guest list."

"Like they checked in under their real names."

"Good point. But they should at least narrow it down to

the dates people checked in. Maybe if I see the list even a fake name will jump out at me."

We watch people moving past, getting on the elevator, getting off, half of them drunk and it's only noon. These Vegas people are brilliant, giving away free alcohol so people can lose their money even faster.

"You really think this dude won't hurt your friend?" MJ asks, startling me because I was so focused on watching the people filing past, hoping I might catch a glimpse of them.

"I don't know for sure. But I didn't get that feeling from him, and I've been around enough scary people to know. Mostly I'm just hoping he won't," I say, realizing that my feeling about Cole might be more wishful thinking than an honest-to-God hunch.

"You didn't get that feeling from Donnell, and he ended up trying to kill you."

"I wasn't seeing him straight," I say, never taking my eyes off the crowd. "When you grow up with a kid, play dodgeball with him and drink his mother's lemonade on a hot day, you figure he won't grow up to kill you."

"I tried to warn you about him."

"I'll listen to you next time."

People keep walking by. I figure the ones who look sober and happy probably just arrived. They're sober because they haven't found out about the free alcohol yet and happy because they still have all their money. Next comes a tour guide trying to yell over the slot machine that has loudly repeated "WHEEL OF FORTUNE" about a thousand times since I sat down next to it. Her group is beyond geriatric, so they're having a hard time hearing her. For that matter, *I'm* having a hard time hearing, and she's standing right in front of me. I'm about to suggest to MJ that we find a quieter spot to run our surveillance when I spot Bethanie and Cole heading for the elevator.

"There they are. Bethanie's okay!" I say, relieved and

happy, but only for a second. "Oh snap, MJ. Lana's still ten minutes away."

"What do we do?"

"We follow them. Bethanie is fine now, but who's to say this is not the day he's going to do something. Even once Lana gets here, she'll have to give the subpoena to the hotel, go over the list. That'll take forever. Let's just follow and we'll call her once we see which floor they get off on."

I'm saying all this to MJ as we walk to the elevator, not noticing that the geriatric tour group has just separated us. It isn't until I'm in the back of the huge elevator and the doors have closed that I realize MJ isn't on with me. It's just me, Cole, Bethanie, and half a retirement home.

Chapter 28

When the elevator doors open on the fifth floor, Bethanie and Cole, who have been silent at the front of the car during the short ride, get off. I'm grateful for the tour group between us because Cole and Bethanie didn't have a clue I was just three feet behind them. I wasn't able to see Bethanie leave the elevator, but Cole was the tallest person onboard, and I definitely saw him leave. As soon as the doors open again, I get off with half the tour group on the tenth floor and look for the nearest stairwell. It takes forever to run down to the fifth floor, and the whole time I wonder why they didn't request a higher level. I'd have expected Bethanie to demand nothing less than a penthouse suite, until I remember Mr. Larsen put a lock on her allowance.

Now that I'm on the fifth floor, I'm not sure what I should do. Call Lana and then stake out the hallway until she gets here? Tell MJ where I am and wait for her so we can confront Cole? Since the first idea is the least confrontational, I go with that one. As I'm dialing Lana's number, I get an idea of how to find Bethanie and Cole's room, assuming they're sharing one. I end the call to Lana and dial the prepaid phone Bethanie last called me from, hoping she hasn't already thrown that one away, too.

I don't hear anything on the first ring so I start walking down the hall, slowing down at each set of doors listening for a ring. On the third ring, I hear something but haven't pinpointed the room when my call goes to voice mail. She's got a nerve ignoring my calls, not that I didn't expect it. Bethanie must know by now that I'm going to curse her out and tell her to get home if she does pick up, which she won't, so I call again.

This time I'm able to tell the exact room the ring is coming from—room 501, north end of the hallway, last room before the door to the stairwell. Cole is smart. He has a fast getaway if the cops—or the bad guys—get between him and the elevator. That also explains the low floor. He could be out of the room and downstairs mixed into the crowd on the casino floor in under a minute. They must be sharing 501 because Cole wouldn't have time to grab Bethanie from another room and make his escape. Amazing how much cops and bad guys think alike.

I listen at the door while I text MJ my location, ready to jump into the stairwell if the voices get close to the door. The voices are muffled, but I do hear Bethanie say my name. She's probably telling Cole who was calling her. I finish the text to MJ and I'm about to start one to Lana when I hear Bethanie scream.

Okay, now what? Run? Panic? No, I'll bang on the door and demand they let me in. So what—Cole can do to me whatever he just did to make Bethanie scream like that? That's when I spot the fire alarm on the wall. I break the thin glass plate with my phone, pull the alarm, and wait on one side of the door, hoping Bethanie and Cole will come out of their rooms like everyone else on the floor is doing. I only have to wait a few seconds before Cole steps out into the hall and looks the opposite direction from where I'm standing, toward the elevator. I take the opportunity to kick him hard as I can in the back of his knees, catching him completely off guard. Now he's on the ground, and probably has no idea what hit him.

Bethanie comes out of the room just as I land my kick.

"Come on, that'll only give us about thirty seconds," I say as I grab her arm and start pulling her toward the elevators. She doesn't put up any resistance, probably because she's still so shocked to find me in Las Vegas, at her hotel door taking down her boyfriend/kidnapper during an apparent fire.

"I thought you weren't supposed to take the elevator in case of fire," Bethanie says. She must be truly dazed and confused if that's the only issue she has with all of this.

"You're right, the elevator is taking too long," I say, wondering why I hadn't used the very escape plan I figured out Cole had come up with. I should have taken the stairs, but now the doors to the stairwells at either end of the hall are jammed with people trying to escape the nonexistent fire. Only problem is I don't see Cole anymore. He must have gone down the stairs with the crowd. The cops can look for him later; at least I have Bethanie, and after I give her a quick once-over, I'm relieved to see she looks fine. I don't know why she screamed, but it looks like the fire alarm stopped Cole from doing whatever he was about to do to her.

Just then, the elevator doors open to reveal two scary-looking dudes.

"That's the guy from the bodega robbery," I say at the very same instant Bethanie says, "That's the guy from my parking spot. You're in the pictures, too. That's how I know you."

I look down the hall and it's now empty in both directions. It's just the bad guys, me, and Bethanie, and I'm really wishing we hadn't just revealed that we know exactly who they both are. That's the kind of thing I hate in movies, and makes me want to yell at the soon-to-be victim how stupid they were for letting the bad guys know they know they're the bad guys. But now I see how it can happen.

Bethanie and I start running toward the stairwell on the other end of the hall, but before we can reach it, the bad guys catch us. Bodega robber has me by the arm, and the other guy has Bethanie.

"Wait, I know who you're looking for," I say.

"We have who we're looking for," says bodega robber.

"You were looking for me?"

"I don't even know who you are," says the other one. "Her—we're looking for her."

Any other time, my feelings might be hurt, but right now I'm more afraid of the bruise bodega man is going to leave on my arm, and probably worse.

"No, I mean Cole. That's who you really want, because he betrayed you and the Family."

The two guys look about as confused as Bethanie. Yeah, that'll teach you not to know who I am.

"Am I right?" I ask, but don't wait for an answer. "Of course I'm right. I left him doubled over in pain in front of room 501. Take him and let us go."

"He ain't there now."

"Because he ran back into the room."

"During a fire?"

"There's no fire. I pulled the alarm, and I told him so."

"DeLong wants the phone. Where is it?" parking spot guy asks Bethanie.

"Cole took it from me," Bethanie says.

Why is everybody and their mother jonesing for her phone? Do they think the cubic zirconium are really diamonds, too?

"Cole also has the ransom," I lie, "and isn't that what you really want—Cole and the money?"

"What's going on, Chanti? What ransom?"

"Shut up, Bethanie. You're just delirious and confused. Cole must have drugged you," I say, but the bad guys aren't buying it.

"Thanks for the tip, but we want Cole, the money, and the girl," says parking spot guy as he starts pulling us down the hall toward room 501. "Since you seem to know so much, we'll need to take you with us, too."

As I'm being dragged to room 501 where Cole certainly is not hiding, I wonder how I'll explain that to the bad guys when we get there. Just then, Cole steps out of the stairwell and yells something I can't make out, but the bodega robber takes off running down the hall. At the same time the parking spot guy lets go of Bethanie to follow his partner, the elevator pings its arrival. I start heading for it, hoping the doors stay open long enough for Bethanie and I to jump on, but Lana and Falcone step out of it. Now they're separating the two bad guys—bodega man between Cole and the cops, and parking spot guy between the cops and us. I can see on her face Lana is working out how she'll run this, but before she can even draw her weapon, the bad guy has already run back to Bethanie and me. His gun was already drawn. He has the advantage.

"Okay, this is how it's gonna go down—" the bad guy starts, but doesn't get to finish.

The only thing that goes down is him. MJ has tackled him from behind and is now sitting on his back and applying a choke hold until Lana can get him into handcuffs. Falcone takes off in the other direction after Cole and bodega man, who are probably long gone, lost in the crowd on the casino floor.

Chapter 29

MJ and I are back in our hotel room, where Lana has posted a local cop outside in the hall in case there are any more bad guys running loose in the hotel. After MJ crept out of the stairwell on the other end of the hall and jumped that guy, I feel safer with her close than I do with an armed officer. I tried to talk Lana into letting Bethanie hang out in the room with us until it was time to return to Denver, but Lana whisked her off someplace to question and debrief her. Lana also knew I'd question Bethanie the minute I got the chance. Since I don't get the chance, I speculate with MJ instead.

"Why do you think everyone was after Bethanie's phone? She was always frantic about knowing where it was, the bad guys wanted it, and Cole took it from her. At first I thought it was diamond-encrusted and everybody wanted to steal and pawn it or something. And it could be that, but I think there's more to it."

"You said her dad's paranoia was at level ten. Maybe that's how he tracked her," MJ suggests. "He used the GPS as part of his home-style version of witness protection. Or the cops did. Then Cole made her get rid of it because he thought everybody, including the Family, might use it to track them."

"That's an excellent theory. See, you'd make a good cop."

MJ is smiling all teeth from the compliment, until the second sentence sinks in. I help her out when I remember something else about the phone.

"But I have a better theory. She lost her phone during the bodega robbery and was in a panic. I jokingly asked if she had some embarrassing photos on her phone and she got kind of mad. When Cole found it and returned it to her, the first thing she checked were her pictures."

"Most people would probably check their messages first," MJ says.

"Exactly. Then when we ran into the bad guys today, Bethanie said something about recognizing one of them from some pictures. She must have photos of something that would incriminate DeLong."

"Or she was using them as protection insurance for her family. But why carry it around, and why not lock the phone if you are gonna carry it around?"

"I think if you're Bethanie and never stay in one place for very long, always having to get out of town quick, you probably think the safest place to keep something valuable is on you. And now that we know who was after her, she probably figured they could hack any password lock."

"Okay, but what I don't get is why Cole thought he was bad enough to double-cross the Family. My contact said he hadn't even been working the game that long," MJ says before she drains the can of 7UP she took from the minibar. After she took out that bad guy, Lana told her to help herself to whatever she wanted out of it, and MJ is doing just that.

"That's just the beginning of my questions for Cole. Right now the only thing I can confirm is that I was right about him setting up that bodega robbery with the other guy who got away. I hope Falcone can find them."

Just then we hear the key card in the door. MJ grabs a lamp from the desk and is ready to do battle, but it's only Lana.

"Whoa, calm down. We've got a man posted at the door. No one's getting in here."

"Yeah, I've seen enough movies to know the man posted at the door always gets taken out," MJ says, unconvinced.

"Exactly—in the *movies,*" Lana reminds MJ.

"What about Cole and the bodega robber?" I ask. "I suppose Falcone lost them in the crowd."

"No, we have them."

"Really? How? I've been in that casino floor crowd. That's how MJ and I got separated in the first place."

"We got them; that's all you need to know."

"I don't see how," I say. "They had a minute jump on Falcone, not to mention Cole is smart. He thinks so much like a cop that I . . ."

Lana is quiet but has that look on her face she gets when she's trying to figure out how much she should say. We both know each other better than anyone, we both read people as well as any psychologist, and we both tend to suspect everything. At times like this, we're less mother and daughter and more like two cons trying to outgame each other. But I already saw her flinch.

Everything starts tying together for me. MJ was right when she said Cole had gotten in with the Family quickly, all *Donnie Brasco*–style.

"He *is* a cop," I say. "Cole is undercover and so is the bodega robber. But for who—Denver or Atlanta?"

"Neither one."

"Mom, I deserve not to be lied to. MJ and I were on point through this whole thing. Y'all wouldn't have solved this case without us."

"I'm not lying to you, if you'd let me finish. And this doesn't go outside this room." She gives MJ the evil eye and MJ nods her agreement. "He's FBI. I didn't know it myself until today. They were involved because of the organized crime with the Family."

"Isn't he a little young for FBI?"

"They recruit agents at twenty-one."

I guess Cole didn't lie about that, at least.

"The Boss is paranoid about taking anyone into his confidence who has been in the game longer than a minute. He doesn't trust the longtimers. The feds wanted someone who appeared young and impressionable to charm DeLong and infiltrate the Family."

"Well, that would be Cole. He charmed a lot of people," I say, running down the list I knew of: that restaurant maître d', the leasing agent, Bethanie, and probably me if I weren't . . . well, *me*."

"Las Vegas FBI have been running this thing for a long time, casting a wider net than DeLong's operation in Atlanta. They started here, but found DeLong's illegal sports book in Atlanta was tied to an organized crime syndicate in Vegas."

"So that's when they recruited Cole," I say, realizing why Cole's accent kept throwing me off. "He really was from around Atlanta because they needed a local to fool DeLong. But he also really went to school in DC where the FBI probably recruited him in the first place, but was based in Las Vegas. Before he went to work for DeLong in Atlanta."

"Not just based here. He started his cover here, as a driver for the Vegas end of DeLong's operation," Lana explains.

"Cole being a cop explains why he came back when things were looking bad for Bethanie and me in the hallway, right before you got out of the elevator."

"He never left. He was waiting in the stairwell, had the door cracked a little so he could watch. His partner, the bodega robber, had let him know they were on the way up, and something was about to go down."

"The bodega robber was undercover feds, too?" MJ asks.

"He was working inside the Vegas operation," Lana says.

"I guess it was a good thing he was able to get the bodega owner to go along with that robbery setup," MJ says, looking at me. "It's sort of like he helped the investigation. Kind of heroic and everything."

I don't care how she spins it, I'm going to eventually have to tell her Eddie might be another bad boyfriend choice. Then it occurs to me what I did to Cole in the hallway.

"Oh no, I can't believe what I did to Cole," I say, cringing with the recollection.

Lana laughs. "You mean with the fire alarm and the kick? He's recovered enough to tell me I have one tough daughter."

"Oh my God, I'm so embarrassed."

"Don't be," Lana says.

"That's right," MJ says. "You did what you had to do. He ain't dead, is he?"

"So why did Bethanie scream?" I ask.

"Scream?"

"That's why I pulled the alarm in the first place. I needed a diversion to get them out of the room because I thought he was hurting her in there."

"I don't know anything about that. You'll have to ask her that yourself when we're back in Denver."

I plan to ask her that and a few other things.

Chapter 30

I had a chance to ask Bethanie that question and more once we were back home. She and her mother were given two days to get their lives in order before they became part of the witness protection program. Well, their old lives. Bethanie was about to begin yet another new life, even though the one she'd been living was only a couple of months old. She'd be the new girl again, hopefully for the last time, or at least for a long time. But not before I gave her something from her reverse bucket list—a birthday party with people other than her parents present.

Mr. Larsen was already somewhere in FBI custody until the trial. But her mother, Tiny, and Molly/Josephine helped me pull the party together quickly at their house without Bethanie even knowing what was going on. That's how big their house is. Of course, we had to make an excuse for Lana not being there since not everyone at the party knows she's a cop, but I was able to invite a few other people even though it was so last minute.

Bethanie didn't have much time to make any friends besides me, so I invited my own—MJ, Tasha, and Michelle. I asked Mildred from school to invite her son Reginald. He'll be starting Langdon after the midterm break thanks to me.

While I was keeping myself out of jail last month, I also busted Headmistress Smythe for wrongly expelling Reginald the year before. I figure he'll need a friend in the viper pit that is Langdon Prep when he returns. People will turn on you at the first sign of adversity. Even Bethanie did that to me before we became real friends.

Marco came, too. Alone, even though I told him he could bring a plus one. A girl has to put up a good front, right? But that hasn't stopped me from paying extra attention to Reginald even if all I can think about is Marco. He's here alone but he's still wearing one of Angelique's friendship bracelets. If I'm capable of stopping a crime family from kidnapping my friend for ransom and taking out an FBI witness, I'm sure I can get over being dumped by a gorgeous, sweet, sexy guy who gave me the best kiss known to all girlkind. Well, I'm reasonably sure.

My phone rings and it's Lana.

"How's the party going?" she asks.

"Pretty good, considering I had about three minutes to throw it together."

"I saw Marco go inside."

"Where are you?"

"I guess you two never made up, huh? You've been watching him since the minute he arrived, but you've barely said a word to him."

"Lana, where are you?"

"Take a look out front. I'm in the cable truck."

I go to a window at the front of the house and spot the truck.

"Doesn't this case belong to the feds now?" I whisper, wondering if one day I'll have to leave the state just to avoid being a surveillance target of my mother.

"I wanted to see this thing through to the end. I've made a few friends; they let me hang out. Feds aren't all bad."

I guess they aren't all humorless, either, because I hear a few laughs in the background.

"So why don't you go talk to him?" she urges.

"His mom hates me, so what's it matter?"

"She doesn't hate you. I've talked to her and she seems nice, just concerned about her kid like any mother. Like me. She and I have the same beef with you, actually."

"I know. You want me to stop playing detective."

"Such an easy thing to do, especially if you really want Marco back."

"I don't think I ever really had him."

"Oh, I'm sure you did. And to be honest, I'm more than happy for you to stay clear of any boy until you're thirty, preferably married first. But I know that's just wishful thinking. If there has to be a boy, Marco seems like the right one. It's obvious you like him."

"We're just friends. Or were."

"Chanti, I'm not clueless. I was your age once."

The minute she says that, our conversation goes from awkward to undoable.

"What was that?" she asks.

"What?"

"That look. And you flinched."

"You've got eyes on me right now? Lana, I need to find Bethanie before she has to leave with your new friends."

"Marco's mom tells me he's seventeen," she says, unde-terred. I turn my back to the window so at least she can't see my reactions anymore.

"So?"

"You're about to be sixteen."

"Okaaay," I say, wondering why Lana is so intrigued by the obvious.

"You and Marco are not me and your father."

"You mean my sperm donor," I say without thinking. It

just slipped out, probably because it's exactly how I feel. And probably because Lana called me on something I hadn't realized myself when I should have been the first to get it.

"I can see why you think of him that way. I do, sort of, except I think of him helping me do the best thing I've ever done. It was the wrong time with the wrong boy, but I wouldn't change a thing because now I have this great kid. She can be a total pain in the behind sometimes, but still great."

"Mom—"

"Chanti, I'm not asking you to repeat what I did. In fact, you better not or I will send my scariest street informant over to talk to your little friend. But you can't be afraid to take chances."

"But you're always saying—"

"I mean take chances with your heart. Not with mobsters and thieves."

I don't tell her Marco is already back with Angelique because it would spoil the mood, I'd probably burst into tears the minute I caught Marco's eye, and what kind of party would that be?

"Only a few minutes until these guys come for Bethanie," Lana says, giving me an out.

I hang up and walk across the room to Bethanie, making sure I avoid running into Marco and Reginald. I don't think I can handle *any* boys after my mother's psychoanalysis, no matter how right she is. When I locate Bethanie, I pull her into the kitchen and away from the party.

"Okay, since I just gave you the best birthday party of your life, you have to answer my questions. All of them, no holding back," I say.

"The whole truth, and nothing but," Bethanie says. "That's what friends do, right?"

"Exactly. First question: I know from the photos and

school stuff on your corkboard you've lived all over the place. But where do you call home?"

"You were right about that one. Atlanta is home. That's where we started, and after years of moving around, we returned there, which is when my dad got involved with DeLong. You made me crazy every time you came close to figuring it out."

"The phone . . . what was up with everybody wanting your phone? I mean, besides the diamonds?"

"Diamonds?" Bethanie asks, looking confused at first, but then she laughs. "Those were zirconias. You think I'd walk around with that many diamonds? I might be rich, but I ain't stupid."

"But it must have had something people wanted, maybe more than diamonds, and you walked around with it. Which—sorry—does seem a little stupid."

Bethanie takes a seat at the bar, the very bar where I first discovered her lottery winnings and where, just a few days ago, she got mad at me and left in a huff. That seems like forever ago, and soon she'll be leaving forever.

"When we were still in Atlanta and DeLong kidnapped me to scare my father, I managed to take pictures of him and some of his men."

"But wouldn't they have taken the phone from you?"

"They did, but I carried two—one for regular stuff, and one for emergencies, the kind only my father could get us into. When that phone rang, I knew it was business."

"Sort of like the Batphone," I say.

"What?"

"Like on *Batman*. The Batphone was only used when all hell was breaking loose in Gotham City. Never mind, just tell me about the pictures."

"They didn't realize I had another phone in a secret pocket on my backpack. I snapped a couple of photos and figured if I ever got out of it, I'd take them to the cops. Keeping the phone on me was the safest place I knew."

"Why didn't you ever go to the police?"

"Going to the cops would also mean exposing my dad to his part in both the illegal gambling and scamming DeLong. We won the lottery soon after and went on the run. I see now it wasn't the brightest move, but without my father knowing, I got word to DeLong that if he ever came after my family, the photos would come out."

"Not a bright move, but definitely badass," I say. "Next question. Did you really like Cole that much, and if so how are you doing now that you know the truth?"

"I really did, and it sucks."

"Details, please," I say. I already knew a lot, but there were holes only Bethanie could fill in.

"Cole was sent by the Family to kidnap me, but his FBI goal was to protect me. When that guy showed up in my parking spot that day, he'd been sent by DeLong to handle the job. Cole was taking too long and DeLong thought maybe he was too much of a rookie to handle it. That morning you saw the two cars leave—one was the bad guy, the other was Cole."

"So Cole started watching your house to figure out your patterns, but ended up watching it to protect you."

"Right. But that morning, he realized DeLong's patience had run out. Cole tried to find the guy and keep a watch on him, at places like the dog and horse tracks, it turns out."

"I was wondering about that. At first I thought Cole was looking for your dad at the tracks, but that didn't make much sense if he knew where you lived."

"But it was too much for Cole to watch me and stay one step ahead of DeLong's dude. That's when he came up with the idea of getting me out of town while the local cops got my dad someplace safe. Since he was based in Las Vegas, and knew they had a wider operation going there, he felt it was safer than Denver."

"Seems like he could have told my . . . I mean the local cops what was up."

"He needed to keep his cover, even with the locals, because the FBI isn't stopping with DeLong. They're hoping to take down the whole Vegas operation."

"But why not tell your family?"

When I ask this, Bethanie looks sad for the first time since we yelled *surprise* to start her party.

"He wasn't sure where my father's allegiance was—to saving me or himself. Not that I blame him."

Without blowing Lana's cover, I tell her what I know is true. "I've spent some time with your dad. He made some bad choices, but his allegiance is completely to you."

Bethanie still looks a little bummed, which is the last thing I wanted to happen at her first real birthday party.

"Okay, last crime-related question. Why did you scream when you were in the hotel room?"

"I was playing in-room Keno and had just won a thousand dollars."

"Seriously? I thought Cole was in there trying to kill you. You have millions of dollars and you screamed like that over a thousand?"

"I've never won anything before. I mean something that was just for me, not a poker game for my dad or a math bowl for my mother."

"How about running? You won medals for that."

"That wasn't about winning. That was getting as close as I could to running away, being free."

"Well, winning a thousand dollars sounds like a perfect reason to scream like you did," I say.

"You didn't ask for any romantic details."

"Didn't think you'd want me to. But I did wonder how

Cole got you to leave town with him. I figured he told you y'all could elope in Vegas or something."

"Close. He never told me that; he just said let's take a road trip and when we stopped in Vegas, I thought that's what was going to happen. Can you believe how stupid that is?"

"You're a romantic."

"I feel like an idiot believing in all that *Romeo and Juliet* stuff. Cole must think I'm a silly child."

"Not at all," Cole says, coming in from the mudroom off the kitchen.

I swear this guy has the best timing ever. I don't know how he does it. I had asked him to try to come if he could. He wasn't there when the party started, but as usual, he's right on time.

"What I think is you're an incredibly brave woman. If you were a year older, I wasn't an undercover agent, and you weren't about to go somewhere far away, things might have been different."

"That's a lot of ifs," Bethanie says, looking a lot less bummed even though the Cole situation is pretty hopeless.

"Yeah, but wherever we're sending you, some guy is going to be so glad we did," Cole says, and then he gives Bethanie something else on her list—a kiss.

It's over before I can turn away and give them a moment, the kind of kiss you might get under the mistletoe when you barely know the boy. But I can tell from the look on Bethanie's face that it's enough to last until that guy wherever she's going discovers her. And then Cole is gone.

"I guess he had to keep his cover," I say.

"Yeah, but he kissed me first."

I let her enjoy that moment a second longer before it starts to feel a little too greeting card.

"All right, one last question. Your parents kept calling you E. Is that code for your real name?"

She hesitates, like she's thinking about whether to tell me.

"No code. I just go by my initial."

"Okay, let me guess," I say, because I love a mystery. "Eve? Elaine?"

"Stop. You'll never guess."

"Edith? Ethel?"

"Echinacea, okay? My name is Echinacea."

"Oh snap. Your parents named you after a cold remedy?"

"It's a flower, a kind of daisy. You wouldn't think anything of calling me Daisy."

"Don't con a con. There's a reason you go by E. Wow. I think I'll keep calling you Bethanie."

"You can't call me Bethanie. After today it won't be my name, and you won't be able to call me at all. Or text. Or visit . . ."

We both forget we're so fierce we survived having a mobster turn his gun on us a day ago and give in to the inevitable hug. Then it really does feel like a greeting card moment, but neither of us care.

The next morning, I decide to go to school even though Lana told me I could stay out one more day. With Bethanie waking up in some undisclosed city and Marco avoiding me, I feel like I'm doing my first day at Langdon Prep all over again. But this time I know I can handle it. The Langdonites, Headmistress Smythe included, no longer intimidate me. In the two months since my first day, I've busted a burglary ring and helped take down a mobster. Rich, self-absorbed preppies I can handle.

Before I head for the bus stop, I sit down at the kitchen table where Lana is having coffee. There's still a loose end we haven't discussed.

"Now that the witnesses and bad guys are all where they're supposed to be, are you going to tell me who you've been trying to avoid the last couple of weeks?"

"What are you talking about? I haven't been trying to avoid anyone."

I remind her of all the phone calls. She stays behind her newspaper, no doubt trying to keep me from reading her face.

"Oh, you mean the bill collectors."

"Bill collectors who also call Papa's house looking for you?" I ask, which finally forces her to put down the A section.

"It's an old debt, something your grandparents cosigned for years ago. It's a debt I don't believe I owe."

I give her a look that lets her know I'm not sold.

"Chanti, it's grown folks' business, nothing you need to worry about."

"I'm not worried. But you are, and nothing ever gets to you."

"Plenty of things get to me."

"But I never know about it. This alleged debt is big enough that I know it's stressing you. That stresses me."

Lana looks at me like she's just seeing me after a long time away.

"Sometimes I forget you're not my little girl anymore. You're half grown now."

"More than half grown. I'll be sixteen in a few weeks."

"Sixteen years. Where did all that time go?" Lana says, looking wistful.

"Mom, I can help you deal with whatever it is—bad debts, bad judgment. No matter what you say, I don't have a monopoly on that. Even parents mess up sometimes."

Something about that comment makes my mother look angry, then sad.

"Don't worry. I'll always be your girl, just not so little."

"I hope that's a promise you can keep," she says, folding the paper carefully. She's thinking of how to say her next words, scaring me a little, and I'm beginning to wish I'd left well enough alone. "Chanti, the person . . . the man who's been calling isn't a perp or my old college boyfriend."

I'm afraid to ask, but I do anyway. "Who is it, then?"

"Your father."

"What?"

"I should have told you before, but I didn't know how. He just took me by surprise; I haven't heard from him since before you were born. I don't know how he found us."

"Where . . . I mean why? Why now?" I stammer. Me, Chanti Evans, finally at a loss for words.

"I don't know. I've refused to talk to him, but I don't imagine it's good. I haven't told you everything about him."

"You haven't told me anything."

"I had good reason, but now it's too dangerous not to tell you."

"Dangerous? Y'all were in high school when you last saw him, just kids crushing on each other, like Marco and me. How does that make him dangerous?"

"Because that isn't the whole story," Lana says, looking more serious than I've ever seen her. "But now he's back."

"Back from where?" I ask, not sure I really want to know.

"Somehow he's back and he's found us and now I have to tell you everything—the truth."

In an instant, I go from ready to take on the world to having my world spin out of control. I want to undo all of my questions, go back to the way it was before the mysterious phone calls began when my biggest worry was busting burglary rings and chasing down a kidnapper. But now it's too late. My life is about to become a lot more complicated.

GIRL DETECTIVE'S GLOSSARY

APB: *abbr.* All Points Bulletin

BOLO: *abbr.* Be On the Lookout

CI: *abbr.* Confidential Informant. Someone who, because of their access to the bad guys, can secretly provide information to the police in exchange for money or a reduced sentence for their own crimes. *slang* snitch, narc

CO: *abbr.* Commanding Officer. A police officer's boss.

defendant: Person charged with a crime by the court.

five-o: *slang* Police officer or detective; comes from the 1970s TV cop show *Hawaii Five-O*, remade in 2010. *also* black and white, po-po, the man

JD: *abbr.* Juvenile Detention. *slang* juvie. **1.** Jail for young people, usually under eighteen. **2.** Where Chanti's friend MJ spent nearly two years before moving to Aurora Avenue.

MO: *abbr.* Modus Operandi. How someone operates or runs their game.

perp: *abbr.* perpetrator. Person suspected of committing or perpetrating a crime.

prosecution: A government's court case against a defendant.

running hot: Police car running with lights and sirens. Cops consider traffic conditions and the nature of the crime when deciding whether to run hot. They generally run hot only when something very bad is happening, like a crime in progress, and getting there fast is critical. If you reported your car broken into, they wouldn't run hot to take your report. If you called 9-1-1 because you hear gunshots being fired, they'd probably run hot. *also* running code, rolling hot

street cop: Patrol officer, as opposed to a detective or ranking officer. *also* beat cop, uniform

vice unit: **1.** Police department unit that usually handles narcotics, prostitution, and gambling crimes. **2.** Where Chanti's mother Lana works undercover.

witness for the prosecution: Person testifying against the defendant, for the prosecution.

CREEPING WITH THE ENEMY

Kimberly Reid

ABOUT THIS GUIDE

The following questions are intended to
enhance your group's reading of
CREEPING WITH THE ENEMY.

DISCUSSION QUESTIONS

1. Chanti is often her own worst frenemy. Sometimes her ability to think like a cop keeps her looking one step ahead, so she misses out on what's happening right now, and overanalyzing situations until she reads into them the wrong meaning. This causes problems in her detective work and in her personal life, as they do with Marco. Do you ever sabotage yourself or your friendships this way?

2. Bethanie feels like she's living her dad's life instead of her own. Have you ever followed a certain path (like planning to be a doctor) or doing an activity (like playing basketball) because that's what your parents want, even though you have zero interest in it? If you could tell your parents what you really feel without them freaking out, what would you say?

3. Chanti says she doesn't feel one way or the other about her father because he was so out of the picture that it's like he never existed. Do you think she really feels this way in her heart of hearts?

4. Cole is a little too mysterious for Chanti, who immediately suspects he isn't who he claims to be. She's a detective-wannabe so suspicion comes naturally to her. How about you—do you trust your instincts when you think something's not quite right about a new person or situation, or do you first give them the benefit of the doubt?

5. When Bethanie asks Chanti to be her cover for her weekend with Cole, Chanti reluctantly agrees, think-

ing Bethanie will do it anyway and at least she'll be in contact with Bethanie. How would you respond to a friend who put you in Chanti's position?

6. Chanti tells Marco he has to accept her the way she is—sleuthing and all—even though it may cost her their relationship. It's true you shouldn't change who you are just to land your crush, but being in a relationship also means compromise. The question is how much do you give up? On this point, are you Team Marco or Team Chanti?

7. When it comes to the truth about Chanti's father, it sounds like Lana has been holding out on Chanti to protect her. Sometimes withholding information about something important is like a lie. Is it okay to lie by omission—even if it's something major—if you're doing it to protect someone? Or do they have a right to know and decide for themselves what to do with the information?

Coming up next . . .

SWEET 16 TO LIFE

A Langdon Prep Novel

Turn the page for a preview of Chanti's next adventure . . .

Chapter 1

I promise. That's the last thing I said to Lana before she left this morning to relieve the detectives working the graveyard shift of a 24/7 stakeout, right after I listed for the third time everything I'd promised to do:

1. Stay out of trouble (I didn't plead my case that trouble finds me, not the other way around).
2. Stop playing amateur detective (I didn't point out how, for an amateur, I'd solved more big cases than she has in the last couple of months).
3. Focus on school and make the most of the opportunity Langdon Prep has given me (I didn't blame Lana for the aforementioned trouble, which mostly happened because she made me go to Langdon in the first place).
4. Choose my friends more carefully (I didn't remind Lana that Bethanie couldn't help it if her father was a crook or that MJ might be an ex-con, but she's saved my butt a few times now).
5. Stay out of grown folks' business.

I plan to keep all of these promises except number five; I was crossing my fingers behind my back on that promise, which is why I didn't complain about the first four. Lana had been hiding something from me for a while now, and a couple of weeks ago she finally admitted the big secret is my father. I prefer to think of him as my sperm donor since that's the first, last, and only thing he has ever brought to the party. He disappeared the minute Lana told him I was on the way. Sixteen years later, he starts calling Lana, and she held out on me about it, pretending he was an annoying bill collector. When it became obvious her threats weren't going to stop the calls, she promised to tell me everything, but so far, the only thing she's copped to is his identity. She got all cryptic about how he's bad news and we don't want him in our lives.

I want to know why because my—let's call him SD for short because the long version is a little too gross to think about more than once—has my mother slightly unhinged and almost nothing has that effect on her. Lana works undercover in the Vice Division where half the job is being unflappable. She can't flinch when a pimp she's investigating threatens her. If some junkie in a crack house she's pretending to live in jumps bad on her because she's claimed his corner of the city-condemned house, Lana has to jump bad right back. She's a third degree black belt in karate and leaves the house for work strapped not once but three times if you include her baton.

So when something has my mother looking over her shoulder, avoiding phone calls at the house, and worse— evading my questions—something is seriously wrong. It was better when I suspected some bad guy she put away years ago was out of jail and making threats. Now that I know it's my SD making Lana this way, it's totally my business and I'm going to figure out what he's about and why he's bringing scary back.

Yep, I'm going to fit that investigation somewhere between getting my grades in shape before finals; wishing my friend Bethanie wasn't in Witness Protection, leaving me to deal with my viper pit of a school on my own; and pretending Marco doesn't break my heart every time I catch a glimpse of him at school, which is all the time and everywhere. Oh yeah, I also need to plan my birthday party. All hell has broken loose since I started my junior year at Langdon Prep, but no matter what happens between now and my birthday, I will be celebrating my Sweet 16 in style.

I'm about to head back to bed when I think I smell smoke. I check the kitchen, but the stove is off, the coffeemaker is cold and I unplug the toaster, just in case. Still smell it. There's no way Lana would have curled her hair just to sit in a surveillance van with her partner all day—even though he is hella cute and she really should make a little more effort—but I check her bathroom for a hot curling iron anyway. Nope, it's cold, too. Then I realize the smell can't be coming from inside because Lana has a smoke detector in every single room of our tiny two-bedroom house.

I follow the smell to the kitchen again and notice the window isn't completely closed. I forgot I'd cracked it open to air out the kitchen last night when I burned the pizza. The smoke is outside somewhere. It's November and definitely fireplace weather, but not before eight o'clock on Sunday morning—people are either still asleep or just starting their coffee brewing. When I step out on the back porch, the smell of burning wood mixed with paint and plastic hits me. Someone's house is on fire. Since I've made the mistake before of calling the fire department when it was just a neighbor's barbecue, I lean over the porch railing and look left, then right. That's when I see the smoke coming from the house two doors down. I grab the fire extinguisher from the kitchen pantry and call 9-1-1 from the cordless phone as I run down the street toward MJ's place.

Chapter 2

By the time I reach the house, the 9-1-1 dispatcher has confirmed MJ's address and told me a truck is on the way. She wants to keep me on the phone—probably because I told her I was going to the house to make sure everyone was awake and out of there—but I hang up on her. I also ignore her attempts to call me back, but not because I'm rude. For one thing, I'm not brave enough to go into a burning house so she doesn't have to worry about that. But I also need the phone to call MJ. It's definitely too early for MJ to be awake, and even her mostly God-fearing, churchgoing grandmother may not be up yet.

While I wait for someone to answer, I run around to the backyard to see how bad the fire is. It's still contained to the porch from what I can tell, but it's starting to snake up the wall the porch shares with the kitchen. Damn—my call goes to voice mail. I run around front to bang on the door, forgetting Big Mama has rejas on every door and window of the house, so all I can do is ring the bell. No one comes.

This whole time I've been carrying the fire extinguisher and somehow forgot I had it. The fire is too big for it to be any use, but it should make a ton of noise if I bang it against the metal bars on the front door. After about thirty seconds of banging the extinguisher against the bars, then dragging it across them, I haven't managed to waken anyone inside the house. A weird thing to worry about at a time like this, but I check the street behind me to see if I've woken up half the neighborhood yet and I'm surprised to find only one person. There's a dude I've never seen before standing across the street in front of Ada Crawford's place. At least I'm pretty sure I've never seen him around, but there isn't much to go on as far as trying to recognize him, since he's wearing sunglasses and a jacket that must be two sizes too big for him because the hoodie covers most of his face. But I can see that he's smiling, and it sends a chill through me.

I go back to ringing the doorbell, feeling completely helpless. It's been about three minutes since I hung up with 9-1-1, and thanks to having a cop for a mother, I know the response time for the nearest firehouse is about four minutes from the time the call is dispatched. They shouldn't be late at this time of day, but what if they are? If I'm wrong and the fire is inside the house, there's been enough time for smoke inhalation to have made anyone asleep inside pass out. I'm trying to decide whether I should slip something through the rejas to break a window and call for MJ and her grand-mother. Since it's November and Big Mama likes to keep her house like an oven, I know there isn't a window open any-where. If the fire has moved into the house and I break a window open, that's only going to accelerate the fire's move-ment from the back of the house to the front. But what do I do? They must be inside—where else would they be this time of day?

That's when I hear the sirens; they are close. In Denver Heights, sirens must be like crickets to people in the sub-urbs—the sound is always there in the background so you never really notice them. But I do today because I've been lis-tening for them, praying they live up to their four-minute re-sponse time. Now I don't have to make a decision about whether to break the window because the fire trucks are on Center Street, less than a quarter mile away. Now I hear them turning onto Aurora Ave. I'm still ringing the doorbell and calling MJ's phone for the umpteenth time when two trucks stop in front of the house.

The first man off the truck runs ups to me while the others begin their work.

"Did you call this in?"

"Yes, sir. Looks like it started around back on the porch," I say.

"Anyone in there?" he asks me while he waves the men around back.

"It's so early, they must be, even though they don't answer the phone or the doorbell. That's their car parked out front."

"How many?"

"Two. Their bedrooms are on that side," I tell him, pointing out the locations. "Probably still asleep. I don't hear any smoke detectors, so maybe the fire hasn't moved inside."

"Or they don't have any. Move over there now," he says, and I go in the direction I think he waved. I'm not sure.

It's starting to sink in that the fire may be worse than I thought and MJ and Big Mama are in there, already passed out from lack of oxygen and every entryway to the house is covered with iron bars. I feel kind of numb—this is all so surreal—but move out of the path of firefighters and hoses. People are starting to come out of their homes, woken by the sirens if not by all my banging and yelling. The strange dude in the hoodie is still standing in Ada's yard, but he's no longer smiling. Now he looks agitated as he stares in the direction of MJ's house, shifting his weight from one foot to another, jiggling his hands inside the pockets of his jacket. He's still wearing dark glasses even though the morning isn't bright at all, and I can only assume he's watching the firefighters work.

Just then, I spot MJ near the end of the block, coming from Center Street. First she's walking, then she starts to jog and then breaks into a full-out run. I meet her one house away so I can try to stop her from trying to get inside. How I expect to stop a girl who has seven inches and seventy pounds on me, I don't know.

"MJ! You're okay."

"Yeah, I was at the bodega. What the hell . . . ?"

"What about Big Mama? They're prying the rejas off now so they can get inside."

"No, she ain't in there. She left last night on a church mission to Grand Junction. No one's in there," MJ says, although it sounds more like a question than a statement.

"Are you sure? We need to tell the firefighters."

"Yeah, I'm sure. Who else would be in there?" she asks, looking over the growing crowd. "They're going to ruin the door. I need to give them the house key."

While MJ goes to talk to a firefighter who looks the least engaged with putting out the fire, I scan the crowd, too. The dude in the hoodie is gone, my friends Tasha and Michelle standing in the spot the probable arsonist was standing just sixty seconds ago. Tasha waves at me; I wave back. Maybe I was crazy and there was never a dude in a hoodie.

Then I spot him, or at least I think it's the guy because I can only see the back of him. He's walking up Aurora Ave toward Center Street. His jacket was solid black when I saw him from the front. Now I see the back is printed in white, some kind of elaborate scroll or vector design. In the middle of the artwork are numbers written in an Old English kind of font, maybe 04. I've never seen a sports jersey where the numbers were so elaborate. And I don't know much about sports, but I've been a groupie at enough of Marco's football games to know they don't use the zero in front of a number. If it's a single digit number, they just use that digit—no zero. He's getting too far away for me to see it clearly, but it's enough of a description to be helpful to the cops.

I look around for MJ so we can follow him. That's something I'd never have the nerve to do, but with MJ—former gang girl, ex-con, and still scary—I'm fearless. But by the time I turn around to make sure the perp is still walking down the Ave, he isn't. He has disappeared.

Chapter 3

MJ is still talking to the firefighter, though it looks more like she's yelling at him. MJ is the most chill person I know besides Lana. As much as they dislike each other, they have a lot in common, like always being cool and under control. I figure MJ must have snapped because the cops have given her some bad news about whatever they found in the house. So I'm surprised when I walk up to them and hear MJ ranting about the basement.

"Our first concern is making sure no one is inside the house, then we can check structural damage," the firefighter is saying.

I'm wondering why he even has to have this conversation when the fire *is still burning.* I think MJ has lost it.

"I told you ain't nobody in there. You need to stop the fire," MJ says, as if a man with the job title of *firefighter* doesn't know that. "It can't reach the basement."

"MJ, come on and let them do their work," I say, but she shakes my hand off her arm.

The fireman looks relieved to see someone sane trying to reason with the crazy girl. "You'd better get your friend out of my face or I'll call the police and have her arrested for obstruction," he warns.

Those are the magic words for MJ in just about any situation. MJ hates the cops and will avoid having to deal with them even when she's freaked by the possibility of her house burning down—or her basement, which has suddenly become so important to her. She even apologizes, or at least gives her version of an apology.

"All that ain't necessary," she says. "I'll just wait over here."

MJ comes with me to stand in Mrs. Jenkins's yard. Mrs. Jenkins lives in the house between mine and MJ's and she's usually fussy about her yard—she'll yell at me if I cross it to get to MJ's place instead of using the sidewalk, and woe to anyone who lets their dog use it for a bathroom, especially if they don't clean up after. Mrs. Jenkins will spy from her living room window all day long to figure out who did it and call the cops since that's against the law. That old lady is no joke. I'm kind of surprised she never had me arrested for trespassing. But Mrs. Jenkins is mellow about us standing in her yard even though she's right there on her porch and she can see us clear as day. Either she's finally showing some sympathy for MJ, or she's afraid of Big Mama. Well, most folks are afraid of Big Mama. And MJ, for that matter.

"MJ, what's all that grief you were giving the fireman?"

"What grief? I wasn't giving no grief. I'm just worried about Big Mama's house, that's all."

"You only seemed worried about the basement."

MJ cuts her eyes at me, then goes back to watching the firemen. I don't say anything for a minute, until one of the firefighters—the only woman working the fire—yells to the man MJ and I had been talking to that it's contained and under control. MJ looks a little relieved, so I figure it's a good time to tell her about Hoodie Dude.

"Maybe we should let that fireman call the police, anyway," I say, and MJ looks at me like I just suggested we kick puppies.

"Not for you. For the arsonist who started this fire."

"I know your mom is one and everything, but you still have way too much love for the cops. Ain't no arsonist started this fire, Chanti."

"When I came down here to wake y'all up, I saw this strange dude standing across the street just watching the house."

"Strange how?"

"Strange because I'd never seen him before."

"Despite you being in everybody's business 24/7, there may be a few people on this block you don't know."

"Like who?" I ask, because we both know that isn't true.

"So he was staring at the house. Half the neighborhood is out here staring at it. People are weird that way. They like to watch fire for some reason."

"Nope. You couldn't see the fire at that point. The only reason I knew your house was on fire and called 9-1-1 was—"

"You called?"

"Yeah, and only because I went out on my back porch and could see smoke coming from the back of your house, but the wind made it trail away from your house, not up above it. A minute later, I was banging on your front door and I know for a fact there was no way anyone could know about that fire from standing in the front of the house."

"Maybe the dude smelled smoke."

"Maybe, but why stare at a particular house when you don't know where the smell is coming from? Most people would look up and down the street, trying to figure out which house it is. He already knew."

MJ turns away from watching the firefighters to look at me for the first time since I told her about Hoodie Dude. She gives me a good hard stare, the kind that has probably made more than a few people pee their pants, but since she's my friend, I'm not so much terrified as concerned. Okay, maybe I'm a little scared.

"Leave it alone, Chanti."

Her voice is so cold that anyone else would definitely leave it alone. But I'm not anyone else. I'm her friend. And as Lana says, I just cannot let well enough alone even when I know that's probably the best course of action.

"Look, Chanti, there is no way we're calling the cops. Big Mama's stuff is in there."

"What stuff?" I ask, thinking I might learn what was in the basement that was so important.

"You know," MJ says, stressing the word *know*.

"I'm pretty sure I don't."

She looks at me like I might be the dumbest person on the planet. Then I get it. She's talking about her grandmother's Numbers operation, an illegal gambling game. Big Mama has been running that pretty much since we moved here, long before Lana became a cop. Lana turns a blind eye to it and acts like she doesn't know, just like she pretends not to know Ada Crawford is a call girl. Lana says they're small fry. Living right under our noses while they operate their business gives her opportunities. She won't tell me more than that, but I always figured she meant more opportunity to catch the bigger fry.

Plus, there's the deal I made with MJ when she learned Lana was an undercover cop—if she kept her cover, Lana would never bust Big Mama. Lana doesn't know about this arrangement, but I always figured as long as Lana was holding out for the big fry, I could delay having that conversation. But I often imagine the day Lana finally busts all the criminals on our street and in my head, it always looks like something from a Matt Damon or Angelina Jolie movie.

"There's *stuff*? I always thought it just involved old grocery store receipts and bar napkins with numbers written on the back of them, the newspaper, and a couple of phone calls made to certain people," I say, stressing the 'certain people' part.

"Believe me, there's stuff. Incriminating stuff."

"Well, I don't want to get Big Mama arrested. Maybe once they clear you to go inside, you can get rid of all the evidence and then call the cops."

"Nobody's calling the cops, including you."

"But this dude could be dangerous, MJ. Houses are like Lay's potato chips to an arsonist—they can't just stop at one. Especially after he's seen how easily these old houses light up."

"I told you—this wasn't arson."

"And not only was he staring at the house," I say, ignoring her protest, "I'm pretty sure he was smiling."

MJ gives me a look that's scarier than the first, if it's even possible.

"Not like that, MJ. He was the opposite of that. You're definitely not smiling."

"'Cause there ain't nothing funny about this."

"Exactly my point. Why would that dude be smiling about something as serious as a fire? We aren't smiling. Nobody on this street is smiling," I say, looking around the crowd, mostly as an excuse not to look at MJ, who I'm sure is thinking of ways to kill me, or at least to shut me up.

"Would you just listen to me when I tell you to leave it alone? And this is the last time I'm telling you to *leave it alone.*"

"But MJ . . ."

"There ain't no arsonist unless you consider me an arsonist."

"What?"

"It was me. I started the fire."